The
Second Chance
and other stories

Alan Sillitoe

SIMON AND SCHUSTER
New York

Published by Simon and Schuster
A Division of Gulf & Western Corporation
Simon & Schuster Building
Rockefeller Center
1230 Avenue of the Americas
New York, New York 10020
Originally published in Great Britain in 1981 by Jonathan Cape, Ltd.
SIMON AND SCHUSTER and colophon are trademarks of Simon & Schuster

Manufactured in the United States of America

10 9 8 7 6 5 4 3 2 1

Library of Congress Cataloging in Publication Data
Sillitoe, Alan.
    The second chance, and other stories.
    I. Title.
PR6037.I55S4   1981   823'.914   80-27643
ISBN 0-671-42761-X

These stories appeared previously as follows:
"Ear to the Ground" and "The Gate of a Great Mansion" in *Bananas;* "A Time
to Keep" on BBC radio; "Confrontation" in *The Guardian;* "The Devil's
Almanack" in the *New Review* and the *Prairie Schooner;* "No Name in the
Street" in *The New Yorker* and the *Nottingham Quarterly;* "The Fiddle" (as
"Harrison's Row") in the *Nottingham Press;* and "The Meeting" in *Punch.*

To H. M. Daleski

Contents

The Second Chance

The
Second Chance

A swathe of Queen Anne's lace was crushed in the front wheelspokes as he pushed along the edge of a field, producing a summer smell pleasant to the nostrils. At the lane he climbed on to the machine and followed the lefthand rut, but when it became too deep and the pedals scraped its sides he balanced along the dry hump in the middle, hitting an occasional stone but staying on track. The thin blue-and-black band of a Royal Air Force pilot officer decorated each sleeve.

The sit-up-and-beg pushbike rattled incurably and had no three-speed. Chalk dust covered his shining toe-caps, but a few quick brushes with a cloth would bring the glisten back. It wouldn't do for the old folks to see him less than impeccable. Why a bike was thought to be more convincing in his approach he did not know. A bull-nosed Morris of the period would have been more in keeping, and in any case he wouldn't have cycled all the way from his airfield, as they liked to imagine.

At the stile he took the War Revision sheet from his

tunic pocket. Major Baxter had folded it in the manner of a trench map from the First World War, so that a gentle pull at two corners brought the whole thing open. Sweat on his forehead cooled under the peaked cap. Dotted lines of the bridle path were clearly marked, but there were no signposts on the lanes. If, as was likely, the old man wielded his field service binoculars from the upstairs window he would already have seen him. He made an observable pause to look at the map before heaving his bike over. To do so was a clause in his instructions, and for the money he had made there was no point in skimping them.

It was an effort to lift the bike without spoiling his uniform but, putting his strength at the saddle and handlebars, he tilted the front wheel to the sky and sent it to the other side. The afternoon visit was preceded by a few hours of intense preparation, mostly the perusal of a refresher course which made him properly familiar with the person he was supposed to be.

He sat on the stile before climbing after his bicycle. White feathers of cirrus in the west were as yet only a wispy tenth or two, but a meteorological front was expected, and his study of such matters led him to predict rain by nightfall. He wasn't to know for sure. Perhaps the storm wouldn't come till tomorrow. There were no weather forecasts on the wireless in the days he was supposed to be living in.

Out of the next field came sharp stuttering cries from a score or so of sheep. The noise of ewes bewailing the loss of their lambs was continuous, and he felt better when the intensity of their distress was lessened by distance.

The old man brought Helen to the window so that they could witness him coming towards the house. At the next corner of the lane he would see them waving when he leaned his bike against a wooden gate and took off his cap to rake a hand through short fair hair. The telegram said he could only stay for tea, but they would be glad enough of that, living in a world where any sight of him could be their last.

'If you must go,' Baxter had said, 'and you must – we all know that, don't we, Helen, my dear? – then don't for God's sake join the army and have to march along those horrible *pavé* roads in France!'

He laughed, as he was meant to while they looked at the hump-haze of the Downs. He was genned up to the eyebrows: 'You don't go from a university air squadron into the infantry!'

Instead of marching at two-and-a-half miles an hour on cobblestones towards the Front as in the olden days Peter had flown at almost a hundred in a Tiger Moth, and later at over three times that in a Spitfire. They welcomed him at the gate as a perfect memorial to their twenty years of happiness – while he knew himself to be nothing of the sort.

Major Baxter found the features so similar, and mannerisms so close when he first noticed him at the bar of the pub-hotel in Saleham that he stood shaking his head as if not wanting to believe what he saw, while knowing it was likely that he would have no say in the matter. The uneasiness of sensing that he should draw back, mixed with a confused vision of what would happen if he did not, vanished like the sort of dream that couldn't be remembered on waking up.

The ordeal of seeing this spitten image of his dead son was so great that he forgot why he had come into the hotel. There was a smell of beer, dusty sunshine and olives (or were they pickled onions?) and a reek of tobacco smoke. He stood and patted the outside of each pocket to locate his cigarette case, which gave time, and saved him being noticed while in a state close to shock. To be caught staring would make him think he'd done something immoral, so he took out a cigarette and had, thank God, to search for a match.

He felt he might be going to faint, and the last time he had known such a sensation was when a shell splinter struck his thigh near Trones Wood in France, too long ago to bother. Having gone unhurt through so many dangers made him also proud of the fact that he'd never been stricken by an illness. Not even as a child had he broken bones or got put to bed.

He turned from his own image in the mirror, hair and moustache silver, tanned face gone pallid. A force that ached in his heels urged him to get set for the door and run, but he was unable to move for the moment, merely telling himself he must not speak to the young man sitting alone at the bar who, if he had worn an R.A.F. officer's uniform with a pilot's white wings on his breast above the left pocket of his tunic, would have been none other than his actual son.

Baxter knew it was useless to say never because no sooner did the word manifest itself than the action began which drove him towards what he had decided not to say or do. To determine never to take a certain course deprived you of that flexibility of mind needed for solving a problem, and laid you open to doing exactly what you had resolved to steer clear of. He knew those 'nevers' all right! A soldier and a man of business had always to be aware and to beware of them. At the same time he realised that, as in every crisis, the necessary action would demand a combination of will, judgment and luck, a trio of factors he had rarely managed more than two of at any one time.

He had come into the hotel because his cigarette case was almost empty. His vigour made him more likely to admit that he had 'seen things'. But he hadn't. Yet having acted, even in so small a fashion, the shock was no longer disabling. To do anything at all would clear at least one part of the mind, and suddenly he found himself as far as the bar.

He was a large man, stout but erect, and a one-handed grip at the rail, vital to his pride, allowed him to appear nonchalant when the waiter came through an archway. The young man who looked like his son spoke before Major Baxter could give his order: 'A pint of your best bitter.'

'Yes, sir.'

'I have the most raging thirst.' When he drew out his wallet and opened it wide to pull a five pound note from an inner pocket Baxter's sharp eye took in the details of a formally lettered business card.

'It's the first hot day of the year,' the waiter said, robbing Baxter of saying the same.

'We waited a long time for a touch of the sun. Always have to in this country, I suppose.' The voice had a tone of lassitude and disappointment which Peter's never could at the age he had died. Yet it made him seem even more as if he might be Peter, who hadn't grown a day older in appearance but who, having seen everyone else put on the years, reflected the fact in his voice.

Baxter stood so that he could see the young man's face in the glass from both angles. Different images shifted and confirmed the exactness. But he questioned whether it was such a likeness, whether he hadn't in the space of twenty years forgotten what his son looked like, and whether the young man merely resembled one of the photographs in the snapshot album.

At sixty-six Baxter recalled how true it was that a few years after Peter's death he had, out of an inner and ever-burning grief, forgotten the precise shape of his son's features. Yet nowadays he was able to see people and events of twenty or even forty years ago with a sharpness that hadn't been possible when nearer to the circumstances themselves. Thus he remembered his son's face as if he had seen him only five minutes before, and knew that it was the same in every part as that of the young man lifting the glass of beer to his mouth.

He asked for cigarettes, and a double whisky so as to make sure his impression was correct, and to convince himself that he wasn't going absolutely bonkers. He had little philosophy of life beyond the injunction to check everything once, twice, and three times – which was periodically necessary if you were to get anywhere, and defend yourself against the world.

'Passing through?'

He knew that the neutral and jovial tone was characteristic of himself. His left hand shook, but was controlled the moment he was aware. He hoped no one would have noticed the inner shaking of veins that led to his fingers. But by holding even his elbow still in its tracks he was afraid the whole limb might turn to stone. He saw his own features, and how the much whitened eyes bulged even more from their sockets, causing him to reflect that he always did look like a bloody fish, with too much eye and bristle.

The young man noted Baxter's smile, as well as his blue and white striped shirt, the grey tie and blue alpaca cardigan, and the heavy black horn-rims that looked like National Health specs but that no doubt cost a bomb-and-three-quarters at some posh opticians. He saw that he had grey hair, a moustache half hiding lips which he thought to be too thin, and deep blue eyes. Small town pubs were full of such lonely old souls, though Peter felt he had nothing to lose by answering:

'Driving to Brighton. I get so thirsty on the road, not to say bored.'

He wore a good jacket, and a shirt without a tie. Wouldn't allow it in the evening, Baxter told himself, even these days – conceding however that he looked smart enough. His hair had the close and even waves that had been in his son's, and was similarly short. He clipped his words in the same way.

'Going there for pleasure?'

He turned, and by laughing at this harmless query fell into the trap Baxter had laid to gain several advantages at once, for while recording the full intensity of the grey-blue eyes, Baxter also got a sight of the teeth, and was able to gauge the tone of the laugh itself, as well as notice how he put slightly more weight on the left foot than the right. He used the word *uncanny* in his summing up because he couldn't think of one that fitted the coincidence more neatly. The shape of the fingers, the motion of the hands, the clean-shaven texture of the skin – were the same.

There was no reason to be unsociable. 'Heavens, no. Stay in Town for *that!*'

During one vacation Baxter's son had spread a navigation chart on the study table to do some plotting practice. He had looked over his shoulder and watched his hands manipulating a pair of dividers, opening and closing parallel rulers, wielding fine-pointed pencils, and dextrously twiddling the knobs of a Dalton computer. The fingers matched those now reaching for matches on the bar, and lighting the same brand of cigarette that his son had smoked.

Hating the nosey parker he had suddenly turned into, Baxter wondered what he could say next in order to delay the young man, who would otherwise finish his pint and motor off to whoever he was going to visit in Brighton, never to do this route again while he would be placed to meet him.

He was saved the trouble: 'It's work I'm bent on. Business, you know.'

'Are you now?'

The matter was left for a moment. Baxter thought
he might offer him a drink, yet saw no point in
keeping him. If he vanished for ever that would be
fate, for both of them, as well as for Helen. He at
least had been vouchsafed another sight of his son,
and mulled on this till he remembered that Helen
might wonder why he was late coming home. She
wouldn't, and never had. When Baxter had come
home that day and heard that Peter was reported
missing presumed killed she was just turned forty,
and had been concerned about nothing and nobody
ever since.

After a long hot day in early autumn Major Baxter
had returned from a field exercise with his Home
Guard company. At forty-six years of age he was
ready, with his good health and experience, to lead
his men once more. Others like him had been in the
trenches, and in defence would have the kind of
staying power that the young couldn't know about.
Nineteen-eighteen seemed like yesterday to those
who had served in France, and they were excellent
stiffening for the others, as well as being good
shots.

Baxter was known as 'Old Scissors', and wore the
faintest of smiles when he got them on parade, or
had them semicircled about him for a lecture, because he knew they didn't realise that he was aware
of his nickname. But they did. There was a point
beyond which he wasn't much bothered, but it took
him deep enough in the association for them to trust
him, and be willing to follow him anywhere providing it wasn't too far towards the besetting sin of
incompetence. He was a good leader, because he
knew how to lead gently. Yet he was more aware of
their limitations than he was of his own, and maybe
that was the reason he was never given a battalion.

He came home exhausted and filthy, yet still excited from his time out of doors, throwing map case, field glasses and tin hat on to the stand in the cool hall. A seventeen year old had broken his ankle leaping a ditch, so he would have to call and see him tomorrow on his way to the office. The damned fool should have waded over, but he was a young bull who could hardly let experience take the place of brains because he hadn't yet got any. God help some of them if the Germans came, though they still had a few tricks tucked into their gaiters.

Helen stared into the food safe.

'Better shut it,' he told her, 'or the flies'll make an entry.'

She didn't turn: 'George, there's a telegram on the table.'

He saw it. 'Open it, then. Must be from your mother.'

'*You* do it.'

Unbuttoning his battledress tunic, he felt an unexplained rage eating at his backbone, as if the ache of two days were attacking him all at once. 'We'll see what it says, shall we?'

'No, don't.'

Her plea went into him like a thorn, but he kept his voice in its proper place, assuming that one of them would have to for the rest of their lives. 'Oh, come now, my love, close that thing, and let's have tea.'

It was as if she had turned to wood. He picked up the small brown envelope. The telegraph boy had known what was written there, and so had she, hands shaking as she scribbled in his receipt book for the telegram which they had dreaded since the war began.

She heard the faint rip as if the sky were being torn in two. 'Please!'

Impossible not to bring out the small piece of

19

folded paper. She sounded as if she would never forgive him if he did, but what he read dimmed all feeling, such pain at least promising that nothing would ever hurt him again. Her eyes told him to say nothing, while he forced her as gently as was in him away from the food safe and into the living room. He obeyed her by not repeating the words of the telegram, and wondered ever afterwards why he had locked the message away with his insurance policies and never looked at it again.

Peter had cycled home a few days before his last sortie over France where he had been killed in his fighter above the towns and villages Baxter knew so well. While Helen slept he looked at his old maps and wondered where it was, but packed them away on hearing the shuffle of her feet as if they were love letters from some liaison which it would break her spirit to learn about.

She said nothing, but his nothing in response was of equal intensity. The perfect union between mother and son had been blighted by death. Baxter's own love, though it was all he had, seemed little by comparison, the sort of nothing that didn't even have anything beyond except nothing. But she didn't say a word, as he recalled, and neither could he, for any speech on the matter would have been so shallow as to have spoiled that ideal love.

The affection between father and son had also been perfect, in its fashion, but different in such a way that it would always remain impossible to define. There was no label for it, and he was not the man to give one, or to try and sort out whatever lay behind it if he did.

Not a tear had dropped from Helen's eyes in over twenty years. He would have liked to have seen some stain marking her cheeks, a sign of pain from which it might be feasible to recover. The thought sometimes occurred that maybe she wept in secret, but there was never any indication to reinforce – let alone confirm – such a suspicion. And if she did, which in spite of having known her so long he still couldn't be certain of, he had no right to venture into such an intensely personal area. Because she never wept, he learned to live without hope, and did so with no complaint.

He watched her hair turning grey, like a flower settling too soon into winter after an unexpectedly bitter frost in August. To anyone looking on, it appeared that she took Peter's death like others stricken in the same way, but the loss fixed her to the day on which the telegram came so that time had no effect on her soul.

Baxter had always imagined that the dead were the lucky ones. They had felt it in the trenches even if the saying had stayed unspoken, a common deception to make their peril more tolerable. But the death in this case had caused those who remained to die and Helen, who had taken the shock too profoundly for it ever to go away, wasn't lucky at all. He couldn't understand it, but had always thought that one day he might. Yet he understood perfectly. The fine balance kept him living, and drudged him along in a state which never failed to make people think that in spite of his occasional cynicisms concerning the uselessness of life, he too was 'putting a good face on it'.

Only half of her lived. Life was unjust to her in that he was able to absorb the shock with what appeared to be his more stoical nature – and perhaps, he sometimes thought, indifference. The heart can take only so much pain, yet it was also as if he had been used to such agony since birth. He was thankful that these deficiencies – if that's what they were – enabled him to provide the vital support. One of them had to, and the unspoken treaty allowed Helen to go on living yet never talk about her son.

Forever locked into each separate fire of deliberate forgetfulness was their only way of never putting Peter out of their minds for a single instant, and kept him more alive than if they had gone through endless seasons of grieving together. It was as if one word about him from either would consign him to a void into which all their memories would inevitably follow, and that was unthinkable.

But he continually pondered on ways of bringing Helen back to life without breaking their sacred pact. She stood in the garden and looked with vacant eyes as the engines of Lancasters or Dakotas or Spitfires sounded overhead. Peter's belongings of watch, spare uniform, trinkets and books came home, which Major Baxter signed for and locked away. A friend motored over with his bicycle, and thank God it was on a day when Helen slept from sheer weakness of body and spirit.

Doing the housework, or walking the garden, she would half faint for no reason. Nothing was diagnosed. For years a girl from the village had to be there if he was not. When the war ended he began to hope that she would one day come out of the near catatonic state into which she seemed locked for ever, but 'missing presumed killed' meant what it said, and there was no grave to set flowers on. She spoke, but used only the barest vocabulary to get through life, and nothing brought her clear of Peter's death, nor looked like doing so.

Music and voices blended from the dining room. The young man clacked his pint glass on the bar. 'Well, I must be going.'

Major Baxter drank his whisky. 'Not much of a meal you had.'

'I prefer to drive at lunch time. Less traffic on the road. I hate cars!'

'We all do. But we drive 'em.'

'Not to mention that twenty-mile red-bricked push out of London – through All-the-Croydons.' Peter looked vacantly at himself in the mirror, then turned away. 'I came via Leatherhead and Box Hill. Longer, but less dreary. I'll have tea later, in any case.'

He didn't care to ask a direct question, but there were occasions when all subtlety must be thrown aside: 'What sort of business are you in?'

Peter would no doubt have grown to show his lack of amusement in the same way: 'Books. The anti-quarian kind. I'm going to Brighton on the off-chance of picking up a few. What do you do?'

'I'm Major Baxter – retired. Was in insurance.'

Peter's face lost all interest. 'Nice.'

'I have a lot of books.'

There was no plan, yet Baxter knew what would happen. The occurrence was packed within the limits of a scheme that was manoeuvring *him*, about which he could do nothing because the will to do, or not to do, had been taken away. It was a new experience, perhaps a necessary one, but he masked the fact that he didn't much like it by telling himself that at least it was happening late in life. Had he been younger, his pride would have spoiled it, while even now, an ever-present inanition might cause him to give in and do nothing.

Peter felt blood coming back into his face at the prospect of finding a well-tooled leather-bound hoard he only dreamed about. But there were probably no more than a few damp novels, a children's encyclopaedia, and a mountain of pulp magazines. He could smell them already. Hose 'em with petrol and apply a match. 'What sort of books?'

'Travel and topography mostly,' Baxter said. 'A few natural history. I sometimes forget what I *have* got. Fair bindings though, most of them. Came from my father, who collected all his life. Didn't have the

23

heart to throw 'em out. But space *is* precious these days.'

It sounded exactly the stuff he was after, but it would be foolish to let the eyes gleam or muscles twitch over it. 'Do you ever think of selling any?'

Major Baxter ordered two whiskies. 'I might be, but look, Peter, why don't you come back and see them – if you're interested. Time is time, and nobody knows that better than I do.'

He recovered quickly from hearing himself called by his own name even before, as far as he knew, he had given it. At least, it was his middle name, the one his mother had used whenever his father wasn't close enough to hear.

He nodded at Baxter's idea, and agreed to follow his car, thinking he might make a fiver or so out of the weird old bloke before the day was finished.

Baxter shopped twice a week, and with all provisions stowed in the boot he purchased flowers from the funny little one-eyed woman who had a stall near the car park. After buying them on two occasions when Helen had been unable to leave her room, he felt he could no longer pass unless he took up a bunch of something. The one-eyed woman expected him to, or hoped he would, and you were obliged, really, to encourage a flower stall, for they were rare enough these days. Unless there were carnations or mimosa it was often unnecessary to buy because Helen managed to grow some blooms each year in the garden. Mostly there wasn't much more he could take, because there was nothing she asked for, and little she appeared to need.

The major was a good leader because he drove with care, some would say slowly, deliberately taking bends and rounding corners he had negotiated for the past thirty years with a calculated sweep just short of stalling. Nevertheless he was amazed at

24

how the little red underslung Morgan stayed in his rear mirror and never wavered.

One part of the winding lane was a green tunnel which opened out before turning a corner into a village. Beyond, he waited at a humpbacked bridge for a couple of cars and a tractor to come over, holding back whether or not he had right of way, because he was the sort of driver who tried to stop everyone else on the road from committing the mistakes he himself might have made if he did not hold his recklessness in firm control.

Peter felt confined for life as part of a two-man bumper-to-bumper traffic queue set in rolling and wooded landscape on an empty road. No wonder we nearly lost the bloody war. There were two places at which it was possible to shoot out and overtake, but on such a narrow lane you could always rely on a souped-up bullet-like Mini to come round a bend at sixty and smash you for dead if you made that kind of move. It was no use anyway because he didn't know where the old man lived. Like all cunning slow coaches he didn't give his address so that, with it pencilled on the map, he might have scooted there by himself and waited at his leisure. Maybe he was a bit cracked, and would lead him a fifty-mile zig-zag before vanishing up the drive of some looney-bin or other. Yet if he had the books he said he had, perhaps it might be possible to pry a few dozen loose before other dealers got there.

'As far as I'm concerned,' his father had said, 'you only have two chances in life. You've had the first, and it landed you in prison.'

The days when he would have stood up for his father were over. Get on your feet for those who can help you, otherwise . . . He held his thumb *down* by the side of the armchair where it wouldn't be seen. 'I only got six months.'

Nearly drove into the old bastard. If he's so mean

over his petrol, or careful of his skin, will he ever sell
a book? A rabbit which ran along the lane suddenly
stood perfectly still with fright, then vanished into
the grassy bank as if part of the tarmac road had
tipped up under its back legs.

'Only?'

'Well, I could have got more.'

'Yes, you'd have been sent down for two years,'
his father shouted, 'if I hadn't paid for a solicitor
and a barrister.' He had to calm himself or his
heart would go splash. 'Cashing cheques with my
forged name on them is all very well, but not other
people's.'

'I served four months – with remission.' Peter
could see the fact running through his father's mind
that some people were very law-abiding in prison,
and that if they were as well-behaved outside they
would never get put into the place.

A second chance was like the second coming:
when it appeared he barely recognised it. Flynn
wanted him for his book business, and even his
father thought it sound enough to spare a few
hundred on. It seemed to offer a better living than
that expensive school had prepared him for, which
had only taught him (and the old bastard put on a
higher moral tone to make his point) to be somebody
he wasn't, so as to get things he had no right to, but
in such a way that he wouldn't be able to keep them.
And if he did bring something off he was bound to
get caught sooner or later – as the silly ass found
when he tried his stunts on a woman who had more
astuteness in her little finger than he'd ever have in
the whole of his underworked backbone.

'If your mother had been alive I don't know what
the hell she would have thought, though God
knows, I don't think she would have cared one way
or the other what you got up to, knowing what she
was herself. When I met her she was pregnant,

though a fat lot I knew. I fell in love with her. The war was on. And I didn't give a damn!'

He'd been drinking whisky at dinner, and was un-aware of the malice in his voice, wouldn't in fact remember next morning, otherwise Peter would have given in to his rage and knocked him down. He rarely got drunk, and was in a good mood, and said he would put money into his 'trading venture' (so as to get me off his hands). He even remembered his promise the following day, by which time Peter felt it was rather too late to floor him for having been so vicious about his mother. Not that, at this turn of events, he still wanted to.

His mother had been dead a long time, and all he remembered were her nightly stories during the war when he was four or five which told of his father flying around the sky and coming to earth in a para-chute of different colours. The tale often brought tears to her eyes, so after the first few tellings its mystery became tedious, and when he told her so, she didn't cry any more. But his father had been away in Scotland sorting out legal queries in the Pay Corps and hadn't flown in aeroplanes at all.

The greenery was rich yet still precise. Garden blossoms stood out delicately clear over the lane. Whenever the road took him to a crest the smokiness towards the horizon kept every detail distinct in the foreground, presaging the season about to break. He was unconcerned with what it might bring because he considered that, in spite of his stint in prison, life hadn't been too bad so far.

'It's five and three-quarter miles exactly,' the major explained before getting into his Austin A40 at the car park, but it already seemed like ten, in the unfamiliar area of sunken and twisting lanes whose short cuts the old bloke must have worked out some time before the Flood.

Major Baxter felt that the squat sports car had

never been anything but set red in his rear mirror and waiting for him to move more quickly. But what was the use of it in this day and age? Still, no one had ever followed with such closeness and precision, though he was certain that Peter's pilot and navigator training would have allowed him to do the same. He had brought him up that way, as well as providing lengthy answers to every question, careful not to hide or mislead, and courteous in those innocent dealings between a father and son who had never spent much time together. He had sent him to schools which kept him out of trouble, so there hadn't been any of that and, as time went on, no gaps where it could have occurred, for he went from public school to university, and then via the air squadron to the volunteer reserve, leaving no periods either of idleness or neglect in which he could have contested the rules they had brought him up to respect. Baxter would have found such a dialogue hard to take, and had been glad of the way of life that helped to make it unthinkable. Whenever his son went back off leave it was as if he were returning to school after the holidays.

They'd had much to be grateful for but, like many such parents, had had to pay for it. In those days no one questioned their duty, probably because it had been so plain that they had neither wanted to – nor been able to.

Helen would be glad to see Peter before he went away as unobtrusively as he had come, for she would notice that he was well, and had grown no older while she had so unduly grieved. Perhaps it had been good that they had not mentioned him to each other these last twenty years, for the shock of seeing him might bring her from the prolonged malaise into which she had retreated. The major had not in that time seen one smile or heard any laughter. Her lips had thinned, the mouth had straightened, the eyes had become dull and her movements slower. She spoke far from easily, yet with his help she kept the house and worked in the garden, so that few would surmise she wasn't living a kind of ordinary life – apart from the occasional breakdown.

They'd never had much to do with neighbours, while other members of the family had died over the years, or been killed in accidents, or in war, or had emigrated, or had become so disaffected for some reason that they didn't come within a hundred miles. Circumstances separated the Baxters from everyone else, and they maintained a dignity towards each other rather than to the rest of the world, thus re-inforcing a feeling that had already been there, but that grew stronger the longer it went on after their son's death.

It was the best way they could find of living normally, though he knew that compared to her former self she had altered so much as to have died. He had married her, and Peter had come into the world, and by this she had been killed. If he had relapsed into a similar death such truths might not have occurred to him but, being the simple man he was, and tending to be proud of it – suggesting that beneath the simplicity lay a complexity of which he was even more proud – he hadn't been able to die in that way. And being the kind of man who wanted the richness of life to return to her, he thought that anything was worth the attempt, and that this dupli-cate of their own son found again and following in his car behind should bring her at least a few moments of joy.

Tyres crunched gently to a stop on familiar gravel. Lifting two laden straw baskets out of the boot he heard a few drops of rain clattering on rose leaves and the roof of the brick garage.

'You're late, dear,' Helen called from the doorway.

He looked up, and noticed an edge of darkening cumulo-nimbus. 'We have a visitor.'

Peter stood by his car. These old well-kept country places could be packed with all sorts of rare gew-gaws.

'Follow me in?' Major Baxter's plea would have been difficult to ignore, though Peter considered doing so, because the tone suggested that, after wasting time, energy and petrol there might not be any books after all. Nevertheless, he asked to carry one of the baskets, not knowing that Baxter had deliberately paused for him to do so after re-calling that his son Peter would have offered no less, for even at twenty he had had enough imagina-tion, as well as a shy sort of kindness, to think of others.

Peter put the basket nonchalantly over the left shoulder and held it in place with his right hand, showing freckles on the back of his wrist. Baxter's wife recognised him by this gesture before seeing his actual features, and her husband, with sharper sight, was close enough to notice that her lips were un-usually tense.

From a distance she looked younger than her husband. She supported herself by the lintel, as if there was some weakness in her legs. Peter also noted the hesitation before she waved, and then called his name – with a smile that recapitulated for Baxter in one fell package the whole twenty years of her deprivation. The pain was intense, but he stead-ied himself while keeping back the vivid recollection of his own lost love.

His anguish did not alter the rate of his slow walk towards her. He didn't know whether to hope she'd see this young man as a stranger who reminded her of Peter, or that she would accept him completely as her one-time son. He didn't know which he wanted more, if indeed he now desired either of them. But her intonation of mother-chiding, suggesting she hadn't seen him for a week or so, hid a lack of awareness about what was happening, her smile at the same time putting her beyond the necessity for such perception.

Her face was unusually pale, and when she repeated his name it sounded like a call for help. 'Peter!'

Since leaving prison he had stiffened his spirit by priding himself that nothing could faze him, though he took it as strange that, like her husband, she had known his name before anyone could have given it to her. When it had happened at the hotel he hadn't liked it at all, but on hearing it from Baxter's wife at the door of their house, he felt pleased at such an agreeable welcome.

Baxter noted that she didn't weep at her son's return, or put her arms around him, or kiss him as if she were aware he'd been away twenty years and that every minute she had gone through enough to break any heart. Perhaps it was just as well. She led him into the house as if she had seen him only the day before.

A stick-and-umbrella stand was made out of an enormously enlarged shot-gun cartridge. 'Curious old thing, isn't it? Picked it up at an auction for a penny or two, years ago,' Baxter told him. 'Thought it would look rather good by the door.' He turned to his wife: 'He's come to see the books' – then followed them cautiously into the living room, as if she might suddenly be blessed with reality and blame him for this deception – though there seemed no chance when she turned to say:

'I do wish you would come home more often, Peter.'

The major smiled, and swung his shoulders back as if standing guard over some truth which he hoped neither of them would ever find. 'Maybe he will.'

The only books were a row of paperbacks on a

window ledge. There was no television, either, though an old wartime one-band wireless set stood on a table by the door. He decided against lighting a cigarette out of an unexpected feeling of respect, as if he had been there before and told it wasn't the thing to do.

'I'm sorry,' he said, 'but I'm kept rather busy.' No apology had ever been easier to make. He hadn't known about their books, so there'd been no point in paying them a call. There was a stench in the place, confirmed when an enormous and obviously neutered tabby lifted itself from behind a copper plant pot, dropped softly to the floor like an over-sized floor-cloth, and padded out of the room as if Peter were an intruder it didn't care to meet.

She peered lengthily at him from a few feet away, and even that didn't cause him the uneasiness it might had she been someone less strange. 'It's nice to be here, though.'

The major coughed. 'We're lucky to see him again – so soon.'

'I hear those planes flying over every night' – she waved towards the ceiling but looked at the floor – 'so I know you're so awfully occupied.'

It was difficult to tell what she saw. Her husband wondered, and stood as though ready to dash forward if she fell. She didn't. It was obvious that the visitor gave her strength. She didn't lean for support any more. Clear vision was on her side. She saw Peter, and if it was only a day since he had last called, it had been the longest she could remember. But some days were like that, and it was difficult to tell what made them so. Here he was, and she decided not to fuss too much. The furniture, curtains and walls looked clearer than for years, and reminded her that perhaps it was time to start cleaning the place, since it wasn't good for her only son to come home to a house that didn't glitter with tidiness.

It was easier to breathe when rain swept against the leaded windows, and now that Peter had come back she made up her mind not to give in to those inner powers that often beset her when he was absent. Occasionally, if the assault was too sudden, she went away to the coast, and George would say: 'You'll be as right as rain in a month.' She knew at such moments that because there was some anguish he could no longer take, she was to be put into an air-conditioned cork-lined box to be alone with her nightmares. When they receded she was allowed to come home, but she wouldn't go there again now that Peter was here. She didn't want to, and even George would not persuade her.

In his civilian clothes Peter looked almost the same as before going into the air force. She thought he must feel better to be out of uniform for a few hours, but wished he would smile, because he'd smiled a great deal as a child when he ran about on his own as if the flat and open garden was a maze to which only he had the key. Extending and complicating the invisible maze over the lawn kept him busy for hours. At each laugh he had worked out new twists and turns, or devised an exit that hadn't been there before, or discovered a quick way into the interior that nobody else had been able to find.

He was adventurous and self-absorbed but, after growing up, became serious and hardly ever smiled, and only laughed at moments when neither of them could see anything amusing, or when he thought he was on his own, as if his maze had been wiped out during the greatest disappointment of his life, which was strange, because nothing like that could have occurred, as far as she remembered. He'd turned into the sober young man they'd hoped for, and what could you expect except unexplainable melancholy with this war going on and on? It was a shame that children were brought up to face such troubles.

'I'll make you some tea,' she said.

A glance was sufficient for him to be able to describe someone afterwards, a method perfected in prison where to fix a person for any length of time might cause a fight. He took in enough of Mrs Baxter to remember her blue jersey and dark blue skirt, and that she had straight short grey hair, somewhat vacuous eyes, and dry pale skin which make-up might have camouflaged if she'd been by any chance expecting him. With such features she had once been a lively and goodlooking woman, but he saw that she was now at large in the territories of a fragmented mind, a state which, however, allowed her to maintain those appearances that she had always known were the height of decorous living.

'Mrs Bruce left us a pot of damson jam yesterday. We can have that for tea. You remember Mrs Bruce, don't you, Peter? She always asks about you.'

There was no need to use his powers of quick recognition in looking at Mrs Baxter, for it was plain that she wanted him to stare at her, though he didn't because it wasn't part of his nature to do what people expected. In any case a too studied gaze might disturb her husband, though he laughed on seeing him flush at the mention of Mrs Bruce, whoever she was, as if his embarrassment would have been the same whether he had slept with her or murdered her.

Baxter wondered how aware Helen was of the amount of time gone since Peter's last appearance. Certainly it wasn't necessary to tax his memory if Peter was supposed to have visited them in previous weeks. But there was no way of knowing, so it was better to let him talk, though what worried him at the moment was that Mrs Bruce had been dead fifteen years.

'Of course I remember her.'

The major's tone was one that he used to put

people at their ease, though his laugh scared him in case it revealed anything. 'Perhaps he'd rather have a sherry. I got two bottles of Dry Sack last week.'

'I shall have to think about it,' she said, causing Peter to smile, which made her believe he was doing so out of affection. He had never found it difficult to endear himself to women, no matter how batty they were. One of his girl friends once took him to meet an old aunt, who had talked in the same outlandish way. In the encounter he had combined impeccable behaviour with an ability to carry on a conversation at cross purposes which won him the confidence of the half-crazed lady yet lost him his girl friend because she saw him, so she said at their parting, as being 'too bloody clever by half'.

'No, George. He'll have *tea*. I know my own son better than you do.'

Her vibrant tone concealed a weakness that neither could go against, and Peter had to tell himself that he had seen Baxter's glance in his direction before realising that he had.

'All right then, dear.'

Helen detected their compliance, and smiled at Peter as if he would show her how happy she might finally be. He was on her side, and would defend her against the dark. He loved her, and his grey-blue eyes were opaque with a concern that would comfort her during any bout of desolation, though it seemed improbable that such could occur now that Peter had come home.

Her glances disturbed him, and he was glad to hear: 'You two go and look at the books, if you must. Afterwards we'll have tea in the dining room. It's such a lovely day!'

Baxter walked along the corridor with shoulders more bent than when they met in town, as if being at home made him older. The house smelled damp, and any books in it had probably gone rotten through being set in shelves against an outside wall. Peter clenched his fists at the idea that he had been tricked into wasting his time, and felt uneasy while following Baxter because he didn't yet know what if any profit he'd find by the end of the day.

'What's the idea, telling her I was your son?'

Baxter's heavily veined hand trembled at the knob as he closed the door. 'Keep your voice down.'

'Tell me what's going on, then.'

'I will, my boy, I will' – his sing-song suggesting he might never be able to. They were in a large study whose furniture, Peter saw, would notch up a fortune in the sale room. The Malcombe shotguns in their case must be worth a thousand. There were no guns finer. The major was delighted to show them, then returned both lovingly to their beds of green velvet. 'I'm afraid she does think you're our son.'

The admission demanded a calm response. 'So I gather.'

A lacquered desk shone with its tiers of many drawers. He'd never seen anything so fine. He walked to a butterfly collection on one of the tables, lifted the lid, and peered at their reminiscent colours. A faint smell of ethyl acetate came out.

Baxter looked over his shoulder, pleased at a common interest that might make them more friendly. It was easy to believe his son had come back, though he fought not to while watching him examine the butterflies as intently as if he really had leapt with swinging net between the bushes. 'He collected those.'

'I did the same, once,' Peter told him. 'Not on this scale, though.'

'We didn't stint him. There are moths, as well. You don't see such things any more.' The major opened a cupboard that went from floor to ceiling, revealing exhibition drawers of shells, birds' eggs, geological specimens and beetles. 'They weren't all yours – his, rather. Collected some myself. That drawer was brought from India. Filled that one on the Nile.'

Peter walked to his books. People didn't usually know how to keep them. A man once took him to see hundreds that were heaped in the corner of a garden shed. The smell of mould was appalling. Some were good titles, but all had been ruined, and the only way to move them was with a shovel – straight into a furnace. These, however, were well-shelved and looked after, so it was only natural to expect difficulty in prising a few loose from the old man. He looked at their spines before Baxter unlocked the glass doors.

'Were these mine, as well?'

He opened a copy of Turton's *Travels on the Rhine* of 1828, fingers touching print and paper, then running across the fresh coloured plates. There was Fitzjohn's *Flora of India*, and a first edition of Goldsmith's *Wonders of Nature*. He reached for Sir Roderick Murchison's *Russia in Europe and the Ural Mountains*, with its coloured maps, plates and sections, published in two royal quarto volumes at eight guineas. God knows what it's worth now, Peter wondered.

Baxter pointed to a first edition of Ford's *Hand-Book of Spain*, which led Peter to see, on the lower shelf, Penrose's magnificent *Principles of Athenian Architecture*, a folio volume with forty plates. He had a client for every book in sight. They would positively slaver at the feel, look and – he wouldn't be surprised – the smell of them.

Baxter's face became momentarily anguished. 'Most of them belonged to your grandfather.'

Peter unusually had some pity for people he knew well, and consequently had more than a little left over for himself, but he had none for Baxter, who

37

would have to accept such dislike as part of their pact. What's more he was unwilling to waste too much time on something which kept him from the sort of idleness he called independence. He could have been in Brighton by now. 'What's in it for me?'

'Some are yours, of course,' Baxter agreed. 'You can browse through others when you come to spend a few hours leave with your mother. The only time she smiles is when you're here.'

'So I gather.'

'It's a great blessing for her to see you after so long. She hasn't looked so well in years.' He spoke slowly in order to make sure there was no misunderstanding, though averting his eyes since to look up would give him the new experience of feeling slightly stupid before his son. He threaded his fingers so firmly together that the knuckles turned white. Then he closed the exhibition case of butterflies, all awareness of what had been decided gone from his face. 'Your mother hasn't had much of a life in the last twenty years, but perhaps things will improve now.'

The heavy books could not be carried safely under his arms. He had a vision of broken spines and scuffed pages – and of Baxter picking them up from the floor. The bargain was no confidence trick, poor old soul. He would defy even his own father to think so – not that it would matter if he did. Perhaps his quaint barrister prejudice about being in trade would lead him to see this little transaction as a more worthwhile manifestation of it. He placed all six books side by side on the table, then walked to the open window where he heard the insects living out their noisy lives under bushes and between grass stalks.

The major, erect and with springing steps, as if pleased that his mind was made up on a matter that had worried him for years, went to the desk and set his gaze at the lefthand column of small drawers. He

didn't need to stare, but was putting on a show,
Peter thought. He counted slowly from the top,
took a small key from his coat pocket, and opened
one:

'Have these.'

Peter had expected something else. 'Why?'

'He smoked them. They came back with his
things.'

'So what?'

'You lit your last but one in the hotel.'

'You're very observant.'

'Yes. It's habit. And training.'

The name was the same, but the label a different
design. The firm had kept up with the times. They
were solid enough as cigarettes, and he rolled one
between his lips in case the paper stuck to his skin. He
didn't like being scrutinised, but wouldn't let it
matter, as he scraped the match towards himself and
looked hard at the flame to make sure it was alive.
The tobacco was dry and tasteless.

When Peter let out the first puff of smoke Major
Baxter saw that unless memory was trying to destroy
his mind with pernicious inaccuracies his son's
gestures were exactly repeated by this stray fellow
who looked so much like him. He had never seen
him light a cigarette without a flicker of distaste for
the whole process curling his lower lip, before going
on to enjoy it more than he should.

Peter pushed certain of his mean thoughts aside
because he had the feeling that Baxter could read
them as clearly as a title page in one of those mint
first editions in the bookcase. He decided to be
careful in handling this piece of luck, and be nice to
the old girl when they went down for tea.

'Come on, Peter, I'll show you to your room.'

He wondered whether Baxter wasn't going barmy
in an unspectacular way, in spite of his cunning
expression. He seemed in thrall to something so

monstrous that Peter wanted to get as far from the house as he could. But the rules of the game lay with Baxter. It would be cowardly to go, and deprive himself of knowing just what they were up to. At the same time he didn't like the fact that his curiosity was becoming even more important than the idea of getting something for nothing. Such a thing had rarely ended in anything except trouble.

Baxter's broad back led him along the corridor, through the dust zone and mothball layer to a converted attic. The studio-type window extending the length of the roof seemed out of character with the rest of the house. A brass telescope on a tripod was placed beside a star-globe, and Peter gripped his hands behind his back so as not to touch its brass framework of co-ordinates. He stood by a table that was covered with maps and drawing instruments.

'I taught him to use maps. Must have been better than me at it, at the end – and that's saying something.' Baxter saw reality in their grid lines and conventional signs, but recalled that his son had mastered their utility more to please him than satisfy any innate love for them. Something had gone wrong over the maps, and he couldn't be sure why, though it didn't seem important now that he had – as it were – come back.

The room had been kept tidy, and he imagined Baxter cleaning it every week. The iron grey-painted bed was made up. A fine-drawn line set out from a point on the plotting chart and ended where no towns were, as if whoever had been guiding his pencil along the ruler had heard a voice calling from downstairs and, Peter thought, having been brought up to instant obedience, had stopped work to answer. He had become a pilot, which was as far as he could get from the infantry of his father. When flying, he was on his own.

Baxter took a Royal Air Force uniform from the wardrobe and laid it along the bed. 'Want to get into that?'

His impulse was to say no, because he too had been brought up to say yes. He had worn a uniform for three years in the cadet force at school. There was also the other garb in prison, whose buttons were made of tin, not brass, and the material was horse-cloth, unlike this smartly tailored well-creased blue with its pilot's white wings and officer's insignia. He took the flap of a front pocket between his fingers, thinking that if he had been twenty years older he would once have worn something similar, though it would probably have been khaki, and knowing his luck he'd have been brewed up in a tank, or dismembered around a mangled gun. 'It's good stuff.'

'Of course it is.' Baxter's sharp tone implied that he ought to realise that they had never given him anything except the best.

There was a school desk in one corner, with an inkwell which must have been regularly filled. The black liquid glittered like the tip of a snake's tail, and he drew back at the old man's voice: 'I'll leave you to spruce up a bit. I expect a good tea's being got ready. Don't forget to bring the cigarettes. And if you'd like to offer one to your mother, that's all right. It sometimes amuses her to refuse!'

He heard Baxter close the door. There was an old portable gramophone, and a pile of seventy-eight records on a separate table. When he tried to turn the handle he found it fully wound. He'd done nothing for himself, whoever he was. Peter fought off a wish to set it spinning and play a tune. There were foxtrots and tangos, and one or two classical piano pieces under the heap.

He again thought of running away, but what was

the point? You always ended by going in circles. In the mirror, he wondered how much longer his lips would conceal the bitterness he felt. But he was happy, while knowing he was trapped. For the price of a few books he was doing a mad old woman a favour.

The uniform fitted, except for a slight pressure at the shoulders. He speculated on what books he would take, and on those he might help himself to on a further visit. Before going down to play his part, like someone who had once fancied himself as an actor, he tried to imagine what sort of person he had been whose uniform he was dressed in. The landscape helped, when he looked out of the enlarged window. The green hill in front was overpowering. Treetops of a copse on either side made a darker smudge, and to the right an unpaved lane led to a thatched farmhouse almost hidden by the thickening vegetation of late spring. Two horses walked across a field, and stopped under a tree to shelter from the rain.

Maybe the other bloke had died with this scenery in mind. He swore, out of pity. Bullets had shattered his plane, a handful of burning coals flung at his back with incredible speed. His parachute hadn't opened, and he had gone like a stone into water, stunned at the impact and dead before getting wet. He had come back to life. Peter smiled at the thought that the sky was his parachute, and would hold him for ever. He had never given in to his father's bullying request that he get his feet on the ground. Perhaps he had taken his mother's story too much to heart.

The black shoes fitted. He pulled them off and walked around the room. He was hungry, a feeling which brought him closer to anger than at any time that day. Had he hated this view, and grown sick of looking at it, before leaving for the last time? He put the shoes on again, though they were stiff from lack of wear.

Baxter nodded towards the stairway. 'He'll be down in a moment or two.'

'Do you think he will?'

He watched her. She had thought of setting tea in the kitchen where Peter had liked to eat as a boy, but Baxter insisted on the dining room because it would be stupid taking Peter's mind back to those pampered days. He used the word 'stupid'. There was a war on, and one had to forget such times. He said 'one' instead of 'we' or 'you'. She had to admit there was no going back, and that she was – they were – lucky to have him here at all with so many boys – well, never coming home again. It wasn't easy to make out why he had reappeared when for some time she had thought him 'missing presumed killed', but here he was and it didn't do to question too much. You must enjoy happiness no matter where it came from, and whatever the explanation might be.

'No, don't call him.'

'Why ever not?'

'Just – don't, George.' She was determined to get her own way. It was so long since she had done so that she couldn't remember when it had last happened. But if she won her point now, it wouldn't matter, except that it wasn't really important. 'He must be tired.' Baxter noticed how embarrassed she was at saying so. 'You know he likes a quiet few minutes in his room, even when he can only spend an hour with us.'

She had made sandwiches, and smiled while altering the position of the cake on the table for the third time. He counted them. She wondered where Peter would sit.

He told her. 'Always by the fire. Even when it isn't lit.'

The photograph on the sideboard was tilted towards the window. There were resemblances in the straight but slightly thin nose, in the same lips and similar forehead. He looked like Helen. But the photograph was of an innocent young man who had loved and respected his parents. He had confided in them, and you couldn't have asked for more than that. Pity he had to die. I didn't hang back for my country, Baxter thought, but if only it had been me rather than him. He sighed, having wished it every time his son had come to mind.

The photograph hadn't been in place for twenty years. They had never mentioned his name. There was no need to. She must have hidden it, and looked at it every day. He hadn't known. There was no reason why he should. Their grief occupied separate regions. He had been deceived. She had once gone to the clinic and forgotten to take one of the many paper bundles, and so had stayed twice as long. Now he knew that it must have contained photographs of Peter.

She was in the kitchen filling the teapot. He heard her trying to get the lid on, so went across the room to pick up the frame. The glass was about to crack in his grip. She would see the blood. He heard the tread of Peter coming along the hall and down the stairs, before the pressure could split his fingers.

She had changed her clothes, Peter saw, wore a white blouse and a pale grey, rather long skirt. Her nails weren't grimy any more. He took the heavy pewter teapot, wondering why her husband had let her fill and then carry it.

Her fingers shook. 'You always were kind.'

Baxter leaned against the chair, and Peter saw him looking at his wife as she walked around the table fussily re-laying it as if nothing would ever be right. Every time her fingers touched a plate her smile made her seem younger.

He felt that Baxter didn't like her smile. It made her look more normal, and therefore unusual. A visitor altered the atmosphere. He was afraid of what lay behind it. Lack of perception meant loss of control. An expression of hesitating tenderness was noticeable in Baxter, as if he saw an unpleasant aspect of her that he'd thought would never come back.

Peter held her chair, then sat down himself. Looking across the table he saw the major nod and smile. The drifting veils of rain had gone, and a shadow-line of sun crossed a pile of magazines in the window. He found it painful to watch her hand shaking when she tried to lift the pot. A trivial upset, such as the dropping of a spoon, would send her back into a state of fragile helplessness.

When he went to her she slapped him playfully away: 'If your mother can't pour you a cup of tea, then what use is she?'

Helen wondered why Baxter was so restless – though it didn't disturb her as much as when he was calm. He found it too peaceful, in fact, and had learned to tread carefully because in such tranquillity conflict was always imminent, and at such moments he thought about war with a touch of passion half concealed. Watching Peter and his wife, he knew there was something vital in life he'd never had, though he wasn't sure exactly what it might have been. Yet he knew that the love he had for his son was greater than Helen's. He smiled at the word 'eternal', and Helen reacted to it as if to mimic him when he turned for a moment from Peter. Whatever he hadn't got, it was obvious that Peter had, and had come back to stop him having to the end, though Baxter was willing to go without so as to give Helen the serenity she hadn't enjoyed for so long. There was nothing he would not do so that one day they would be able to talk about their dead son. But

he was begining to see that everything had its
price.

He had learned in prison how to get secrets out of the
walls, how to see through windows that did not
exist, so it was easy to surmise, walking around the
trap of his namesake's room, where the hide-outs of
a tormented mind could be located. The diary rested
on a ledge up the chimney, wrapped in layers of
brown paper and pushed into the sort of canvas bag
in which he took his gym shoes to school.

Careful not to pull down soot or pebbles, he
carried it to the open window and shook the grit
away. There had been no cause to start it before
August, but after so many years he could smell his
elemental panic through the faint pencilling when he
did: 'Mummy and Daddy turned her away. I didn't
write to them beforehand because I knew they would,
though I had hoped they wouldn't. I can't believe it,
but it's happened, so I have to. They didn't say why,
but were quite firm about it as soon as they saw her. I
didn't have the opportunity to tell them what she
meant to me, but it wouldn't have made any difference if I had. I'm sure of it, but it doesn't make me
feel any better.'

No fires had been lit in the grate. Such comfort
might have spoiled him. Everything instead had
been lavished on hobbies and education, which made
the chimney a good place in which to keep his diary.

He read her full name scripted vertically down the
page of half a week: Cynthia Weston, common
enough, with probably a few in every phone book in
the country. Some days after her visit, and before
Pilot Officer Baxter went 'missing, presumed killed'
there were more entries, but Peter was called down
before he could read them. At the major's shout he
anxiously placed the diary back in the soot, and

stood up to make sure there was no sign of it on his uniform.

His mouth was half full of chicken-paste sandwich. Even the tea was good. No teabags here.

'Saw a couple of Heinkel One-elevens over France yesterday. Got one of them at twelve thousand feet. A cannon shell scraped my starboard aileron, but there was no trouble getting back.'

'It must be dreadful, for those poor French people,' she commented.

Baxter grunted. 'Didn't feel much for them in the last war.'

Her torment lasted till Peter came again, but on some visits she was uncertain who he was, and had to make up her mind whether or not to acknowledge that he was Peter whom she thought she had lost. The more hesitation, the greater her fuss when she did recognise him – Baxter had observed. At her distressed moments she knew him from his walk rather than his face. Sometimes he didn't even look like his photograph, poor boy, which was because he worried so much. The war seemed as if it would go on for ever.

'It looked beautiful from up there, those fields spinning under me. I saw the Heinkel hit the deck before any parachutes came out. Sorry about it, though.' He had practised reducing his smile to a look of ruefulness. 'I hate killing.'

'Didn't we all?' Baxter added that he knew those fields. 'We drove around there before the war. Don't you remember?'

'They were wonderful days,' Helen said. 'But so short.'

'On our way to the Loire.' Baxter usually smoked cigarettes, but occasionally lit a short well-worn meerschaum. He calmly released smoke away from the table: 'Stayed the night in Bapaume. Showed you my old sector on the Somme.'

Peter was tired of watching them adore each other, and suspected they only indulged in it when he was in the house. 'Of course I remember. I found a piece of shrapnel by the lane that led to the War Memorial.'

Baxter looked at him with suspicion, yet was grateful for such sharpness, with its hint of generosity towards his mother. Must have seen it in the drawer of *his* room. 'You've still got it, I suppose?'

'It's in my desk upstairs, wrapped in cotton wool, in a tobacco tin with an old ten franc piece.' There was no use denying anything. They could have whatever part of him they wanted – except that which would not even share its secrets with himself.

'You're too thin. I do wish you'd eat more.' Helen spoke as if all her troubles would be over if only his appetite improved.

He lit a cigarette with the crested silver lighter found on the bedside table. The flint had lost its roughage, but went at the second go. 'I'm really too full for anything else.'

Baxter disapproved of him having left nothing unturned in Peter's room. Peter smiled. Of course he had been through his things. What did he expect? Neither of them could dispute that they belonged to him.

'In the last war we couldn't get enough to eat,' Baxter said.

To get into a Spitfire and spill around the sky at over three hundred miles an hour was the perfect antidote to such a home life. Every take-off was a farewell. They hadn't even got his ashes back, not an ounce of salt or soil, only an ex-jailbird and con-man a score of years later to remind them of him. He touched her wrist, and picked up another sandwich. 'You're right. They're so good.'

'Your old school phoned the other day,' Baxter remarked, as if he too must play his part.

Helen poured more tea with a steady hand. 'They were really glad to hear about your adventures.'

'The headmaster read your letter to the boys.'

The notion of having grown up to become a credit to his school, not to mention a prime example of self-sacrifice, pleased him in a way he didn't like, though he put in: 'I only wrote what I felt. I just thought they'd like to hear from me.'

'You made them so happy,' she said. 'And us.'

However convincing he was, the little play had gone on long enough for today. The pendulum clock ticked sanely by the doorway. Didn't she know who he was? It was hard to imagine it could be otherwise. He felt sorry for her, but she wasn't the first person in the history of the world to have lost an only son. When he was fourteen a friend's cousin had run from the garden gate to be struck dead by a speeding car. He was an only child. His mother was a grey shadow, walking the streets but avoiding everyone when she could. She felt no offence when dodged in turn by those who saw her as too stricken for them to say anything that would make either them or her remember it without embarrassment. They were abashed at their helplessness, and she was too agonised to believe that any verbal contact would comfort her, or indeed that she would ever be sane again. Six months later she was working as a secretary in a solicitor's office – thinner, greyer, yet willing to talk about her disaster.

He fastened the top button of his tunic. 'I'll collect my books, and then I absolutely must be away.'

Her disappointment was easy to cover with a smile. A cake was packed in a box. I'll throw it out of the car. Every time he left there was a cake in a bloody box. The bow came undone as she put it on the table. But she retied it before the major could get up to do so – as she had known he would.

Baxter handed him his card by the door: 'Telephone when you can come again,' he whispered. 'Make it as soon as possible.' He had written his request on the back also, and there was a similarity to the sharp cramped handwriting in the diary. He put it in his flap pocket. Peter had no longer been a young man when he had scribbled those last entries.

He saw himself telling his tale in a Notting Hill pub. I've got this batty old pair who think I'm their pilot officer son killed in the war. He couldn't, though it was hard to give up what laughs he might get. Baxter admired his car:

'New one, isn't it?'

'I borrowed it' – he loosened his tie, and threw his cap on to the back seat – 'from the adjutant.'

A few more visits would complete his tour of operations. He'd often decided not to call on them again, not even for the cupboard of toys he had discovered under the stairs. He had taken away one or two that wouldn't look amiss in an antique shop window. But the Baxters had been different from his own parents in their treatment of the son they had once had, because they had kept all he'd ever possessed. *His* father had flung everything out when he'd gone to prison.

Baxter was whistling some idiot song from the thirties as he stood at the stove cooking breakfast. He stopped as soon as he was aware of Peter's approach, and glanced at his undone tunic. When nothing came of it he went to work with the spatula to prevent bacon and sausages burning. 'Did you have a good sleep?'

Peter lit a cigarette, to cut the pungent smell of smoking fat. 'Marvellous, thanks.'

'The air's fresh down here, that's why. There are cornflakes over there. Sauce. Bread. Butter. Marmalade. All you need.' Every time he stayed overnight he was given the same instructions, as if he was never expected to learn. 'Grapefruit you'll find on the dresser.'

Whenever he had gone so deeply into sleep he wasn't hungry for breakfast, yet took one of the leathery, stained eggs on to his plate while Baxter sat to a meal of scorched streaky and broken sausages, surrounding it with blobs of sauce and dabs of mustard, as if laying out picquets against wily enemies waiting to launch a surprise assault from the wilds of Waziristan. When he suggested they go shooting that afternoon it was merely his way of giving Peter the morning to himself. 'We'll take the Malcombes.'

'All right.'

Baxter put both plates in the sink. 'Doesn't hurt to use them now and again. We might get a rabbit, or a pigeon if we're lucky. There's not much else around these parts.'

There was peace in the house, until an aggressive banging of church bells from the village began. The unholy assault on his senses as he wandered around the garden was so intense that he went up to his room and lay on the bed to look through the diary of his last year alive. A large greenish fly lifted into a zig-zag course before he brought a hand close to turn the page.

'I don't much care whether I live or die. In fact it would be easy for me to make sure of the latter.' The last entry came soon after, and he was disappointed that there was so little to read: 'Back to the squadron! I can't wait. Better there than here. More bang-on sport, the only sort I like.'

At lunch every button of his uniform was shining and fastened. He laid his cap carefully on the dresser, and as soon as Helen ladled the soup he said: 'I'm having trouble paying my mess bills these days.'

Baxter stopped eating, eyes flashing behind his glasses, as if the shock was greater precisely because he had expected it, and he was now uncertain how to respond. Peter couldn't decide whether he was the most devious bloke in the world, or the most dense. 'I'm afraid a few awkward questions are going to be asked.'

During the long pause Baxter's face assumed a blank expression, and became as sunburned as if he'd done another stretch in India. He was about to speak, but reached for his glass of lager, grunted, and drank off half of it.

Helen's hand lifted, and she looked at Peter. 'You must have been very careless.'

'I believe I was.'

'We shall have to help you' – though speaking as if she at least wouldn't mind.

'I'm sorry. It's an awful situation. But I need three hundred quid immediately. I'd hate the wing commander to find out.'

'You should damn well watch your mess bills,' Baxter grumbled. 'Take better care of things.'

He wanted to laugh at him squirming like a snail on a nail. 'I'll try – from now on.'

'It's easy to run 'em up, but hard to pay when the time comes.'

'I'm sure he *will* try,' said Helen.

The glare was steady with disapproval, but Baxter felt too unsure of himself to say much more than: 'Will he, though?'

Such well-contained rage could be ignored. 'I might.'

'You will, won't you, Peter?'

He hadn't stopped eating, so they couldn't complain about his lack of appetite. 'I'll have a go.'

It had been a gamble, though he'd enjoyed the risk, which seemed almost as good sport as going after the clumsy old Stukas. Top-hole, in fact.

'He's such a nice young man, isn't he, dear?' Helen said, breaking the silence.

Baxter thought he might as well get something out of the situation, so looked as if unwilling to emerge from his sulk. 'Who?'

'Don't be silly, dear. You know who!'

She's never been deceived, Peter thought. She won't tell, either. It's Baxter who's deluded, though it'll make no difference in the end.

Baxter climbed a stile and moved across the meadow with the training and care of a lifetime. A couple of prime rabbits, ears at the sky, neither heard nor saw him. Peter stood fifty yards behind, aware that he would be hopeless in the matter. Two shots were so rapid that the noise rolled into one. Both rabbits spun on the grass, and Baxter ran from one to the other, stilling each with a chop at the neck.

'Damned good cat meat.' He wiped specks of vivid blood from his glasses, then put the empty cartridges into his game-bag with the rabbits.

In spite of his flying boots, he went forward more silently, but on squeezing the trigger found to his chagrin that he had forgotten to push off the safety catch. He felt better, however, when he fetched a couple of pigeons down: 'I'll get my batman to roast 'em on the spit!'

'You should. You seem to pay him enough.' Baxter was unwilling to call him a robber outright. 'I suppose you lost money at cards?'

Peter reloaded. 'It'll help pay my rent.'

'Or on women. That sort of thing.'

'Not at all.'

'Go on, you can tell *me*.'

The wind had strengthened and changed direction. They couldn't get into the lee of it without wading the stream. 'I owe a packet on my car. Don't want them to fetch it back.'

'Mess bills are sacred. You should lay something by. Wouldn't hurt. Apart from showing the white feather, it's the worst thing out.'

He put the safety catch on. The temptation to become involved in the creation of a fatal accident was too great. 'I'll try to be more economical, but I'm afraid I'll have to come back for more if things keep getting out of hand.'

Peter watched him moving up the lane, game-bag slung too low behind, gun crooked in his arm, head looking to left and right as if dreading an ambush. By the dark copse he turned a corner, too angry to want his company on the way home.

He need never see them again, yet a new-found formality with regard to Mrs Baxter contained a certain amount of pity, and he decided to make a few more visits. He couldn't yet walk off with one of the Malcombe guns, though hoped to before the appropriate goodbye.

A voice grated into his ear like a file pulled across balsa wood. 'Peter?'

'It's the middle of the night, for God's sake.'

'It's me – Baxter. And it's nearly midday.'

The curtains were thin, and let in sufficient light for him to see his watch. God knows how he'd found the number. Maybe he'd followed him, or had him followed. Perhaps he'd searched his car while he'd been in Peter's room looking for more secrets, or gone through his things in Peter's room while he had been talking to Helen in the garden. But he'd never let them out of his sight or sound. 'What do you want?'

He saw Baxter in a phone booth near the market, just off the High Street, a pile of coins neatly stacked on the Bakelite shelf. Couldn't phone from home in case Helen heard. 'Your mother wonders when you're coming down for a day or two?'

Peter's lips were ready to shape obscenities at his pleading tone, but decided they were too good to waste at such a distance. 'Don't know when I can.'

'We'll be glad to see you. You know that. Don't you?'

His head ached, and he wanted breakfast to sop up the whisky he had been drinking till four o'clock. After days of intense work compiling a catalogue of their best books, many of which came from Baxter's choice collection, he felt the need of a long rest. 'Do I?'

'Can't you wangle a bit of leave? Even thirty-six hours?'

He hadn't been to see them for a fortnight, being tired of acting the part of their long lost son. When you found such easy plunder you were never far from being caught, so jump – before the axe fell. He put some encouragement into his voice: 'I'll see what I can do.'

His speech droned on through his hangover: 'Ask the C.O. He'll let you have it. I remember him. He's a very good chap. I'm convinced he will.'

Still holding the telephone, he got out of bed and walked to the window, drawing back the curtains to let in daylight. 'I expect you're right,' he interrupted, trying not to laugh. 'He's such a ripping sport!'

Baxter chuckled. 'He won't refuse one of his best pilots.'

He lodged the receiver under his chin while lighting a cigarette. 'How did you find my number?'

'What number?'

How dense can the silly old bastard get? 'Telephone number,' he shouted.

'Oh, looked it up in the book. But don't forget. Come down and see your mother. She's not well.'

The pushbike idea was too much like hard work, but he'd agreed because Baxter did deserve some consideration after having parted with over a thousand pounds. He swore when his ankle caught on the pedals. Nor was the bike much good for carrying valuable old tomes in the saddlebag to his car parked at the station nearly six miles away.

He opened the War Revision map sheet with Baxter's name scrawled in pencil along the top margin. The folds were torn after much use. It was not necessary any more, but Peter had cycled home on his last visit and used a similar map which, so Baxter insisted, he always carried even though he knew every lane and stile around.

When a piece of grit lodged in his left shoe he leaned the bicycle against a bush and scooped it clear with his thumb. There was a gap in the hedge. Damp soil, pocked by cow hoofprints, was scattered with bits of dead twig. He screwed up the map and slung it there.

At the lane a fat youth went by on a motorbike whose noise seemed to tear the heart out of the countryside. Peter glanced at the bulbous pale cheeks under a red helmet, and the hunched body dead-set towards the village. He mounted his push-bike and pedalled the last few hundred yards.

They stood at the gate like an advertisement for a life of happy savers and insurance payers. He thought Baxter's arm was around her, but couldn't be sure. When he was close he saw them wave.

'I shan't be seeing you for a long time.' They strolled back and forth on the lawn. 'The squadron will be packing up for the Middle East soon. I can't tell you exactly when, because it's very hush-hush.'

The major's eyes suggested he'd already said too much. Didn't he know that rhododendrons had ears? He looked nervously towards the hedge, and then at Helen who said:

'We know you can't, dear.'

Brambles were growing outwards from the trees. The end of May had seen thunderous weather and a few hot days, and huge white Queen Anne's lace – as well as nettles – had become too tall to stand upright. The place looked more ragged than when he'd first seen it. 'There'll be promotion, though. Another step up.'

Baxter liked the idea. 'Be nice if you could reach squadron leader before it's over.'

If the war dragged on he might even get to wing commander, which would be one rank above major. Peter supposed it wouldn't do at all from Baxter's point of view.

'We'd be very proud if you did.' Her dress was too long, but she was smart and self-confident these days, and he was sorry for her that it was about to end.

The major walked with a stick. He wore a panama hat and a pale light jacket. 'We must mow the lawn sometime, Peter. Tidy things up a bit.'

His uniform was too hot, and he unbuttoned the tunic. A black-edged cloud which the met bods hadn't warned him about stood in the west. If Baxter grumbled at him for being improperly dressed he would tell him what to do with himself. Helen's ready smile made him think that she knew what was in his mind. Bad show. He had taken the diary home months ago, and there wasn't a word he didn't know by heart.

He sat on a straight-backed chair in the cool living room. Baxter made a jug of lemonade, and Peter hoped he'd splash in some gin. He didn't. The cat spread itself across a magazine on the window ledge like an old wine skin, and closed its eyes. Helen's smile disconcerted him because it didn't quite fit what she was saying. She sat with folded hands. 'I pray to God you'll be all right when you go overseas.'

'See a bit of the desert, mother. Have to brush up my navigation.'

Baxter put down his lemonade glass. His voice quavered. 'He'll do his duty, as we did in the last war.'

'I know he will.'

She wasn't absolutely sure, so he said: 'No worry on that score.'

He would have had no option except to have done it, yet knew that if he had to do it today he would be most unwilling, though to perform one's duty might at least help to pass the time. But the need for that sort of duty had not yet come, and probably never would till it overwhelmed him whether he wanted it to or not. He refused to let it concern him while there was an issue to be settled which did not conform to their ideas of duty at all.

'Mother, I wonder if you mind listening to me for a moment.' He heard his own voice with the same detachment as when he first spoke to Baxter in the pub. Since that meeting times had changed, though he wasn't sure by how much. The idea that under certain circumstances he would be like Baxter when he got to his age frightened him, and gave him the courage to go on: 'I have something to tell you.'

His sharp tone caused her to look up with an expression which asked who was this stranger in her house? Her son's face was grey. The features shifted from her, but when she smiled, as she must if the life she enjoyed with him was to remain, they came back, and his face turned pale again. He always appeared as if exhausted, and she wondered what was wrong. Something surely was. The more she saw of him the more he looked like she felt. She wasn't his mother for nothing.

Peter hadn't heard such a laugh before, but Baxter had. Every time she looked at George, even when the three of them were happy together, he seemed afraid of something. But she didn't think it sufficient reason for Peter's face to turn into that of an ashen-visaged young man so close to death. She would try not to laugh again like that.

'Do you remember when I brought Cynthia home?'

'Who?'

George's hand lifted in a half secret motion meant for him alone.

'You remember. Both of you do.'

'Cynthia? Now, let me see . . . '

'You wouldn't let her stay.'

Peter was missing and presumed gone for ever. That trivial incident with Cynthia had only been known to the three of them. He had neither written nor telephoned for a month. The uncertainty had been appalling, but the agony of his death had erased the memory of those weeks. He had put a call through to his commanding officer, and when Peter did come back, nothing was said about Cynthia. Everyone had been sensibly forgiving.

He'd read the lines so often it was easy to speak them: '"Met Cynthia. This is the real beginning of my life. I know I'll never be happier."'

'What's that?'

'The secret thoughts of your one and only son. You brought me up to rely on you for everything, but when I came to see you with my girl you turned her away as if she were a . . . ' His voice was about to break, and he thought tears already marked his cheeks, but pride stopped him lifting his hand to find out. 'I was open in those days, even honest, in spite of the war. There wasn't much else for me to do except get killed.'

Baxter filled his pipe, but laid it on the table unlit. He thought it only common sense to remind him that such a thing might have happened anyway, at which Helen hoped he wouldn't speak again for the rest of his life.

'It needn't. A lot came through it.' He smiled in the same resigned way as on the day they had made their feelings clear about *that* girl. It was the only time they had seen compliance with their wishes mixed with the bitterest despair. He was able to bring it back any time he liked.

'She wasn't our sort. We told you so at the time.'

'You did, but I was in love with her.'

Baxter stood up, and reminded him that he was pushing things just a little too far. There was no knowing to what lengths a jailbird and confidence trickster would go, however. On days when Helen had looked her normal self he often decided to tell him not to come back. It would be safe then to bring out that telegram (thirteenth drawer down from the right) and show her the news that Peter was missing and presumed to have been killed. He would say that if life was finished, then it was at an end for both of them. But it was clearly too late to do anything now.

'I wrote another letter to my school.' It was impossible to strike one without the other. When Cynthia appeared, she was turned away because they wanted him as much as possible to themselves in his last few months. By not seeing how vital his love affair was, they drove him more quickly to his death. They had let him down, one might say, but more fool he for thinking his parents would do anything else.

Baxter hoped he was mistaken at such malice. 'To your school?'

A photograph at home had shown him standing at attention in front of the cadet force armoury door, on which it said: 'England expects that every man will do his duty.' He was surprised not to have found something similar of Baxter's son upstairs. 'Yes, to my old corrupting school.'

With Baxter, self-preservation meant assuming an air of unthinking optimism. He recalled how, when

Peter at other times had threatened to reveal something, he had made them even more proud of their perfect son by a last second divergence from it. 'They'll be delighted to hear from you.'

'Don't you want to know what I wrote?' He didn't altogether like this side of Peter's revenge. There seemed to be something of his namesake in him, after all. He much preferred to act the good son than indulge in the reality of his true self.

Baxter knew they had brought Peter up in such a way that he would surely have forgiven them if he had really come back to life. 'Don't listen to him.'

Helen saw her son, yet not her son. 'What's changed you, Peter?'

'I'm not your son.'

'You are. You always will be.'

He wanted to leave, but couldn't till he'd made them acknowledge what they had done. 'I told that pompous headmaster what a vicious little bastard I'd really been. I had great fun making a list of dirty books I'd read, and the money I stole, and equipment I wrecked and let others take the blame for. I explained how I hated the war, and all that crap about dying for one's country.'

Baxter's eyebrows lifted as if jerked by an invisible thread. Such a person shouldn't be allowed to live. 'Have you finished?'

'I listened to *you* often enough. It's my turn now. I died cursing, and throwing your stale lies back into your face. I'm not Peter. George talked me into it. Didn't you, George? He played a trick on you, Helen, though he doesn't know what stunts I worked on him when I came to see you while he was in town shopping. We had some good talks then, didn't we?'

She played into the game, and held his arm. 'We did, George.'

He wondered what other lies to tell. Baxter was too

old to strike. A force of lightning would stab back at him. 'Don't go, major.'

Baxter was able to keep calm as long as any trouble stayed within the expectations of an uneventful life. He tried to remain immobile, to hold the pose for ever but saw, in enormous magnification, a shell going into the breech of a gun. It was big enough for a man to be encapsulated in the package. He shook his head at such a ridiculous picture.

'Peter's dead, but he could have got back to base after his last flight. His fuselage was riddled with bullets, but he was only injured. He rammed his plane into the Channel because his only thought was to end it all. I'll keep his uniform as a memento, and his diary, but I suppose you ought to have these.'

He worked his nails under a tip of his pilot's wings, and tore them off. They hit the table, and fell on to the floor.

Baxter knew that the end had come when, at the lowest point of unmistakable decline, he decided that something had to be done to prevent absolute disaster. Too late or not, you still had to act in order to maintain your self-resepct, no matter what the consequences. He picked up the wings, looked at them for a moment, then put them in his pocket and walked away.

He had never left them alone together, and she stood up as if to make the most of it. 'You're not well.'

The truth he had spoken sounded so despicable that he wished everything unsaid. A window had been left open. Wind shook the curtains, and the huge tabby cat jumped on to the ledge with a skinned rabbit leg in its mouth. He wanted to hear her say that Peter was finally dead, but she slumped back in the chair, her clarity dispersed as suddenly as it had come. The expression of despair startled him so much that he was unable to go over and comfort her. The right ascension denied itself absolutely. He couldn't walk away, either. Silence and stillness seemed the only safe possibility.

She made an effort, and spoke: 'We did the best we could – whatever went wrong. You'll do the same with your children.'

The cat was busy on the floor, and he pushed it from the raw meat. Helen flinched: 'Baxter never understood me. It wasn't his fault. He's not the sort of man to understand what's going on. I didn't know how to tell him, but if I had he might have changed so absolutely from the man I knew that it would have made things harder. I needed the person I already knew to help me through the terrors I hadn't known about up to then. Without being aware of it he passed *some* of his on to *me*.'

'I've nothing more to say.'

'Don't be sorry.'

'I'm not. I'm afraid.'

Baxter's footsteps sounded overhead, then the noise of his firm tread down the stairs. Every movement in the house could be heard from every other place in it. Peter didn't know from which way he would appear. The clarity he had forced Helen into brought more pain than he could bear, so the only thing left was to make his way back to the station on foot, crossing fields where normal air existed.

He said that he must go, and she agreed but hoped he'd come and see them again. He nodded to say he would, but she didn't believe him. He turned around, and hesitated when facing the hall door, a preliminary to his movement which was so slight as to seem almost a mannerism, and he was still in the living room when Baxter levelled his gun from the bottom of the stairs.

There was no need to aim. At such short range Baxter would scare him out of his wits so that he would never show his face in the district again – no mean feat with a foulmouthed plunderer who had taken their books and money. And neither would Helen expect him to come back after witnessing the comic antics of his departure. He had fouled her suffering, though he blamed himself for having lured him home that day. It was impossible to say what had happened during the making of a decision for which he could recall no clear feeling of responsibility. Such things happened in life – or they had with him. The same mechanism occurred again when, unconscious of any movement, and in no way making up his mind, he pushed the safety catch forward and pressed the trigger.

The glimpse of George lifting his gun reminded her of one summer's dawn when she had seen him stalk a rabbit that had been ravaging the kitchen garden. He had got up specially, and in the first light he went inch by inch towards the spot where the rabbit quite plainly plundered the carrot tops and rows of peas, secure in its vandalising gluttony. It must have taken him twenty minutes to get close – he in thrall to the rabbit and Helen fixed by him – before he risked a shot. She had never been able to observe him for so long without him talking to her or being aware that she was looking.

Peter stood, his hand at the cold door knob that had to be turned. He didn't want to go, but Helen suddenly urged him to *run*, her shriek striking the back of his neck:

'No, don't! George!'

The agony of her cry forced him to turn. Her eyes were closed, as if she didn't want to know who he was. He was given no time to consider the many reasons why this was so. She fastened her arms on him. Looking over her head he saw the levelled gun, and heard it become the end point of an exploding cone which knocked them against the door and covered his stung hands in blood.

The weight deadened his pain and enabled him to
stay on his feet. She clung so hard that he couldn't
hear what she was saying. The hand tore his uniform
as he let her fall. The pain was like ice. Her burden
smelled of death.

He wanted to say no, don't shoot, you have
nothing to kill *me* for. His mouth wouldn't shape any
words, as if he hadn't enough breath, and when he
knew that he was helpless before the fact that there
was nothing left to live for, he said: 'All right, then,
kill me.'

Major Baxter turned his head slowly left and right,
remembering something that had to be done, a
minor item from long ago that it would be best to do
now in case he forgot until the time came when it
would be too late, as it was bound to if he didn't do it
this minute, a piece of outstanding business that no
one knew about except himself but which tormented
him because the matter had been pending for so
long.

An awkward reversing of the unfired barrel pulled
the woollen tie loose from the folds of his jacket. The
agony that would not let him talk produced only a
simper. There was no atonement for what they had
done. His lips were pursed: given time, he would
break into a mindless whistling of some tune that
would be familiar to all who heard it. He was taken
by a sudden concentration of mind that nothing
could break, and within it his placid expression said:
yes, life is like this, and isn't the world a damned silly
place to be in? an assertion he profoundly believed at
the moment the explosion spread a volcanic crater
backwards and changed his look to one which
showed him trying to eat the moon.

A thunderclap rattled the windows. Peter curled
on the floor. The sound pushed itself deeply in and
then vanished as pellets of shot grazed his skin. The
wind roared through a fever. His fever turned to ice-

cold. Silence when the wind died made him feel he was resting on the ocean bed. Teeth bit into his finger ends. He heard Helen groan, and telephoned to get help.

He had been visiting them. He often did. They were like grandparents. There was a quarrel which he never did quite understand. Got somewhat bitter, though. Hard to say why exactly. The old major tried to frighten him. Yes, that was it. To frighten *them*, if you like. He was fond of them both, and they normally got on very well. Can't think what came over him. Baxter's gun went off when he knocked against the stair rail. He must have slipped, dammit. Certainly didn't mean to shoot his wife, but when he did – by accident – he was so appalled that he killed himself. Who wouldn't be? Eh? The R.A.F. uniform was a fad of theirs. He had been trying it on. They liked him to, occasionally, because it gave them a glimpse of their dead son, whom they said he resembled. Harmless enough, really.

The house and everything else would be his one day. The sooner the better, he told himself. Even the beautiful pair of Malcombe guns. No facts were altered. Can't trim facts. To backtrack by dead reckoning and try to find out how it had come about would not help, no matter how much he pondered. Nor could any inbuilt technological amanuensis have fixed it with any kind of precision. A square-search was out of the question. Interception problems were beyond his competence. Perhaps the triangle of velocities would help, or the probability of errors. But he didn't want to know. There was no purpose in knowing. Silence was freedom now that chaos had turned into order.

He was left with whatever ruins had been thrust upon him while he sat in the living room cleaning Baxter's guns – getting them ready over and over again in case that dreadful book-stealing con-man whose pictures were framed all over the house ever came back. He relaxed his stance only when Helen called from her wheelchair in the garden to remind him that they were going to a party in half an hour, and hadn't he better check the car and make sure that all was ready for him to get her into it?

'I will, my sweet,' he said, and whistled some mindless tune as he went outside.

No Name
in the Street

'Do you know, you get on my bloody nerves, you do.'

Albert's black-and-white dog ran between his feet, making him scuffle out of the way in case he should tread on it and commit an injury. 'You've got on my bleddy nerves all day.'

It was almost dark when they set out for the golf course. A cool wind carried a whiff of hay from large square bales scattered about the field like tank-traps in the war when, as a youth in the Home Guard, he used to run from one to another with a rifle in his hand. It smelled good, the air did. He hadn't noticed in those distant days whether it had smelled good or not. Or perhaps he didn't remember. But you could tell it had been a hot day today because even though the wind had a bit of an edge to it the whiff of hay was warm. 'You do, you get on my bleddy nerves.'

The dog quickened its pace, as if a bit more liveliness would mend matters. And Albert length-ened his stride, not in response to the dog but because he always did when he made that turning in the lane and saw the wood's dark shape abutting the golf course. His dog anticipated this further increase of speed. Having been pulled in off the street a couple of years ago when it was starving, it couldn't afford not to. Even a dog knew that nothing was certain in life.

They'd come this way on most nights since, so there was no reason why it shouldn't know what to do. Why it got on his nerves so much he'd no idea, but what else could you expect from a dog?

'Get away from my feet, will yer?' His voice was little more than a sharp whisper because they were so near. The 'will yer?' – which he added with a certain amount of threat and venom – caused the dog to rub against his trousers and bounce off, then continue walking, almost in step despite both sets of legs still perilously close. 'You'll drive me up the pole, yer will. My nerves are all to bits.'

It wasn't a cold evening, following a hot day at the end of June, but he wore a long dark blue overcoat, a white nylon scarf, and a bowler hat, more because he was familiar with them than to keep warm. He felt protected and alive inside his best clothes, and in any case he usually put them on when he left the house in the evening, out of some half surfaced notion that if anything happened so that he couldn't get back home then at least he would be in clothes that would last a while, or fetch a bob or two at the ragshop if he had to sell 'em.

There was no reason why he should be this way, but that didn't make it less real. Apart from which, he couldn't go to the golf course wearing his shabby stuff. The adage that if you dressed smart you *did* well was about the only useful advice his father had ever tried to tell him, though it was so obvious a truth that it would have made no difference had he kept his trap shut, especially since neither he nor his father had ever done well at anything in their lives.

'Here we are, you aggravating bogger.' He stopped at the fence, then turned to the dog which, as always at this point, and for reasons best known to itself, hung back. 'Don't forget to follow me in – or I'll put me boot in your soup-box.'

No hole was visible, but Albert knew exactly where it was. He got down on his haunches, shuffled forwards, and lifted a strand of smooth wire. The dog saw him vanish. When he stood up in the total blackness of the wood, he heard the dog whine because it was still on the wrong side of the fence.

It showed no sign of coming through to join him, even though it was a job so much easier for a dog than a man. At least you might have thought so, but the bleddy thing was as deaf as a haddock when it came to telling it what to do. It hesitated so long that, after a suitable curse, Albert's pale bony hand at the end of his clothed arm at last appeared under the fence, grabbed it by the collar (you had to give the damned thing a collar, or somebody else might take it in) and yanked it through, briars and all.

It didn't yelp. Whatever happened was no more than it expected. 'You get on my bleddy nerves,' Albert said, holding its wet nose close, and staring into its opaque apologetic eyes.

When he walked along the invisible path he knew that the dog was obediently following. They went through the same haffle-and-caffle every time, and it got on his nerves no end, but it would have chafed them even more if the dog had done as it was supposed to do, because in that case Albert might not even know it was there. And then there would be no proof that he had any nerves at all worth getting on. He often told himself that there was at least some advantage in having such a mongrel.

He could do this zig-zag walk without cracking twigs, but the dog rustled and sniffled enough for both of them, biting leaves as if there was a rat or

ferret under every twig. On first bringing the tike
into his house it had shivered in a corner for three
days. Then one morning it got up, jumped on to the
table (treading its muddy paws all over the cloth) and
ate his pot of geraniums almost down to the stubs.
Afterwards it was sick on the lino. Then he gave it
some bread and milk, followed by a bowl of soup
(oxtail) – and from that point on there was no holding it. He even had to get a key to the food cupboard.

Albert hadn't felt right since his mother died three
years ago, unable to work after losing her, finding
that nobody would set him on at any job because
they saw in his face that the guts had been knocked
out of him. That's what he thought it was, and when
he told them at the Welfare that he felt he was on the
scrapheap, they gave him money to keep the house
and himself going.

It wasn't a bleddy sight. The dog was eating him
out of house and home. Every time he had a slice of
bread-and-marmalade he had to cut some for the dog
as well. Same when he poured a cup of tea, he had to
put a saucerful on the floor. So you had to do
summat to earn a few bob extra.

There was a bit of light in the wood now they'd got
used to it, and when he reached the fence he saw
that the moon was coming. It wasn't much of one,
but it would be a help – without being too much of a
hindrance. Sandpit holes in the golf course beyond
glowed like craters. The dog ran into a bush, and
came out more quickly than he'd expected, nudging
his leg with something hard in its jaws. Albert bent
down and felt cold saliva as he took it and put it into
his pocket. 'That's one, any road. Let's hope there'll
be plenty more.'

Occasionally when they found one so early it
ended up a bad harvest. But you never knew. Life
was full of surprises, and dreams. He had visions of

coming across more lost golf balls than he could carry, pyramids that would need a wheelbarrow to take away. He saw a sandy depression of the golf course levelled off with them. He even had the odd picture of emerging from the wood and spotting a dozen or so, plain and white under the moon, and watching himself dart over the greenery, pocketing each one. In his dream though, the golf balls seemed soft and warm in his fingers as he slipped them into his topcoat pocket.

The dog brought another while he smoked a fag, but ten minutes went by without any more. 'All right,' he said, 'we'd better go and see what we can find. Best not get too close to the clubhouse: the boggers stay up boozing late enough in that cosy place they've got.'

His dog agreed, went through the fence this time even before Albert had finished muttering, glad to be in the open again. They said next door that his mother had to die sometime. Not much else they could say, being as she was nearly eighty. She used to talk to him about his father, who had gone to work one day twenty-five years ago complaining of pains in his stomach, and not come back alive. Something about a ruptured ulcer, or maybe it was cancer. There was no point in caring, once it had happened. The doctor had been kind, but told them nothing – a man who looked at you with the sort of glittering eyes that didn't expect you to ask questions.

Then *she* went as well. He bent down one morning to look, and saw that she'd never wake up. He sat with her a few minutes before going to get the doctor, not realising till he got out of the door that he'd been with her ten hours in that long moment, and that dusk was begining to glow up the cold street.

He was glad to be in the actual golf course because the wood was full of nettles, and brambles twisting all over the place. Stark moonlight shone on the grass so that it looked like frost. Even before he'd gone five yards the dog came leaping back, and pushed another ball into his hand, the sand still gritty on its nose. That was three already, so maybe a jackpot-night was coming up, though he didn't like to think so, in case it wasn't. Perhaps he should hope it would turn out rotten, then every find would be encouraging, though at the same time he'd feel a bit of a cheat if he ended up with loads. Yet he'd also be more glad than if he'd hoped it would finish well and it turned out lousy. He'd appear foolish sooner than lose his dream, though he'd rather lose his dream if it meant things seeming too uncomfortably real. The best thing was, like always, not to forecast anything, and see what happened.

Every golf ball meant fifteen pence in his pocket from the secondhand shop, and some weeks his finds added up to a couple of quid on top of his Social Security. He earned more by it than when he used to hang around caddying as a youth of fourteen before the war. Every little had helped in those far-off days, but there'd been too many others at it. Things had altered for the better when he'd got taken on at Gedling Pit, because as well as getting work he was exempted from the army.

After the funeral he sat in the house wearing his best suit, and wondering what would happen to him now. Going for a walk in the milk-and-water sunshine he wandered near the golf course one day and saw a ball lying at his feet when he stopped to light a cigarette. He picked it up, took it home, and put it in a cut-glass bowl on the dresser. Later he went back looking for more.

He ran his fingers over the hard indented pattern, brushing off sand grains and grass blades as they went along. It was an ordinary night, after all, because they found no more than four. 'Come on,

73

then, you slack bogger,' he said to the dog. 'Let's be off, or you'll be getting on my nerves again!'

'It's a good dog,' he said, sitting at a table with his half pint of ale, 'but it gets on my nerves a bit too much at times.'

They wondered what nerves he had to get on, such an odd-looking well-wrapped up fifty year old whose little Jack Russell dog had followed him in. One of the railwaymen at the bar jokingly remarked that the dog was like a walking snowball with a stump of wood up its arse.

Albert sat brushing his bowler hat with his right-hand sleeve, making an anti-clockwise motion around the crown and brim. Those who'd known him for years could see how suffering had thinned his face, lined his forehead, and deepened the vulnerable look in his eyes. Yet they wouldn't have admitted that he had anything to suffer about. Hadn't he got house, grub, clothes, half pint, and even a dog? But whatever it was, the expression and the features (by now you couldn't tell where one ended and the other began) made him seem wiser and gentler than he was, certainly a different man to the knockabout young collier he'd been up to not too long ago.

He indicated the dog: 'He's got his uses, though.'

The railwayman held up a crisp from his packet, and the animal waited for it to drop. 'As long as it's obedient. That's all you want from a dog.'

'It'll have your hand off, if you don't drop that crisp,' Albert told him. The railwayman took the hint, and let it fall under a stool. The crunch was heard, because everyone was listening for it.

'As long as it's faithful, as well,' a woman at the next table put in.

You were never alone with a dog, he thought. Everybody was bound to remark on it before long.

'A dog's got to be faithful to its owner,' she said. 'It'll be obedient all right, if it's faithful.'

'It's a help to me,' Albert admitted, 'even though it does get on my nerves.'

'Nerves!' she called out. 'What nerves? You ain't got *nerves*, have you?'

She'd tricked him squarely, by hinting that some disease like worms was gnawing at his insides.

'I'm not mental, if that's what you mean.' Since he didn't know from her voice whether she was friendly or not, he looked at her more closely, smiling that she had to scoff at his nerves before his eyes became interested in her.

The dog came back from its crisp. 'Gerrunder!' he told it harshly, to prove that his nerves were as strong as the next person's.

Her homely laugh let him know that such a thing as strong nerves might certainly be possible with him, after all. She had a short drink of gin or vodka in front of her, and a large flat white handbag. There was also an ashtray on the table at which she flicked ash from her cigarette, even when there seemed to be none on its feeble glow, as if trying to throw the large ring on her finger into that place as well. Her opened brown fur coat showed a violet blouse underneath. He'd always found it hard to tell a woman's age, but in this case thought that, with such short greying hair fluffed up over her head, she must be about fifty.

'Let him know who's boss,' she said.

He felt the golf balls in this overcoat pocket. 'I expect he wants his supper. I'll be getting him home soon.'

Her hard jaw was less noticeable when she spoke. 'Don't let him run your life.'

'He don't do that. But he's fussy.'

He observed that she had mischief in her eyes as well as in her words. '*I'll* say it is. Are you a local man?'

'Have been all my life,' he told her.

She stood up. 'I'll have another gin before I go. Keeps me warm when I get to bed.'

He watched her stop at the one-armed bandit, stare at the fruit signs as if to read her fortune there, then put a couple of shillings through the mill. Losing, she jerked her head, and ordered the drinks, then said something to the men at the bar that made them laugh.

'You needn't a done that,' Albert said, when she set a pint of best bitter down for him. 'I never have more than half a jar.'

He needed it, by the look of him, this funny-seeming bloke whom she couldn't quite fathom – which was rare for her when it came to men. She was intrigued by the reason for him being set apart from the rest of them in the pub. It was obvious a mile off that he lived alone, but he tried to keep himself smart, all the same, and that was rare.

She pushed the jar an inch closer. 'It'll do you good. Didn't you ever get away in the army?'

'No.'

'Most men did.'

The dog nudged his leg, but he ignored it. Piss on the floor if you've got to. He'd go home when he was ready. 'I was a collier, and missed all that.'

She drank her gin in one quick flush. 'No use nursing it. I only have a couple, though. I kept a boarding house in Yarmouth for twenty years. Now I'm back in Nottingham. I sometimes wonder why I came back.'

'You must like it,' he suggested.

'I do. And I don't.' She saw the dog nudge him this time. 'Has it got worms, or something?'

'Not on the hasty-pudding he gets from me. He's a bit nervous, though. I expect that's why he gets on my nerves.'

He hadn't touched his pint.

'Aren't you going to have that?'

'I can't sup all of it.'

She thought he was only joking. 'I'll bet you did at one time.'

When his face came alive it took ten years off his age, she noticed.

He laughed. 'I did, an' all!'

'I'll drink it, if you don't.'

'You're welcome.' He smiled at the way she was bossing him, and picked up the jar of ale to drink.

Sometimes, when it was too wet and dreary to go to the golf course he'd sit for hours in the dark, the dog by his side to be conveniently cursed for grating his nerves whenever it scratched or shifted. At such times he might not know whether to go across the yard for a piss or get up and make a cup of tea. But occasionally he'd put the light on for a moment and take twenty pence from under the tea-caddy on the scullery shelf, and go to the pub for a drink before closing time.

If he'd cashed his Social Security cheque that day and he saw Alice there, he'd offer to get her a drink. Once, when she accepted, she said to him afterwards: 'Why don't we live together?'

He didn't answer, not knowing whether he was more surprised at being asked by her, or at the idea of it at all. But he walked her home that night. In the autumn when she went back to his place with him she said: 'You've got to live in my house. It's bigger than yours.' You couldn't expect her to sound much different after donkeys' years landladying in Yarmouth.

'My mother died here.' He poured her another cup of tea. 'I've lived all my life at 28 Hinks Street!'

'All the more reason to get shut on it.'

That was as maybe. He loved the house, and the thought of having to leave was real pain. He'd be even less of a man without the house. Yet he felt an urge to get out of it, all the same.

'So if you want to come,' she said, not taking sugar because it spoiled the taste of her cigarette, 'you can. I mean what I say. I'm not flighty Fanny Fernacker-pan!'

He looked doubtful, and asked himself exactly who the hell she might be. 'I didn't say you was.'

She wondered when he was going to put the light on, whether or no he was saving on the electricity. He hadn't got a telly, and the old wireless on the sideboard had a hole in its face. A dead valve had dust on it. Dust on all of us. She'd picked a winner all right, but didn't she always? The place looked clean enough, except it stank of the dog a bit. 'Not me, I'm not.'

'There's not only me, though,' he said. 'There's two of us.'

She took another Craven 'A' from her handbag, and dropped the match in her saucer, since it seemed he didn't use ashtrays. 'You mean your dog?'

He nodded.

Smoke went towards the mantelshelf. 'There's two of *us*, as well.'

Here was a surprise. If she'd got a dog they'd have to call it off. He was almost glad to hear it. Or perhaps it was a cat. 'Who's that, then?'

'My son, Raymond. He's twenty-two, and not carat-gold, either. He's a rough diamond, you might say, but a good lad – at heart.'

She saw she'd frightened him, but it was better now than later. 'He's the apple of my eye,' she went on, 'but not so much that *you* can't come in and make a go of it with me. With your dog as well, if you like.'

If I like! What sort of language was that? He was glad he'd asked her to come to his house after the pub, otherwise he wouldn't know where to put his face, the way she was talking. 'The dog's only a bit o' summat I picked off the street, but I wouldn't part with him. He's been company, I suppose.'

'Bring him. There's room. But I've always wanted a man about the house, and I've never had one.' Not for long enough, anyway. She told him she might not be much to look at (though he hadn't properly considered that, yet) but that she *had* been at one time, when she'd worked as a typist at the stocking factory. It hadn't done her much good because the gaffer had got her pregnant. O yes, she'd known he was married, and that he was only playing about, and why not? It was good to get a bit of fun out of life, and was nice while it lasted.

He'd been generous, in the circumstances. A lot of men would have slived off, but not him. He'd paid for everything and bought her a house at Yarmouth (where he'd taken her the first weekend they'd slept together: she didn't hide what she meant) so that she could run it as a boarding house and support herself. The money for Raymond came separate, monthly till he was sixteen. She saved and scraped and invested for twenty years, and had a tidy bit put by, though she'd got a job again now, because she didn't have enough to be a lady of leisure, and in any case everybody should earn their keep, so worked as a receptionist at a motoring school. I like having a job, I mean, I wouldn't be very interesting without a job, would I? Raymond works at the Argus Factory on a centre lathe – not a capstan lathe, because anybody can work one of them after an hour – but a proper big centre lathe. She'd seen it when she went in one day to tell the foreman he'd be off for a while with bronchitis – and to collect his wages. He was a clever lad at mechanics and engineering, even if he had left school at sixteen. He made fag lighters and candlesticks and doorknobs on the Q.T.

He could see that she liked to talk, to say what she wanted out of life, and to tell how she'd got where she was – wherever *that* was. But he liked her, so it must have been somewhere. When she talked she seemed to be in some other world, but he knew she wouldn't be feeling so free and enjoying it so much if he hadn't been sitting in front to take most of it in. She'd had a busy life, but wanted somebody to listen to her, and to look as if what she was saying meant something to them both. He could do that right enough, because hadn't he been listening to himself all his life? Be a change hearing somebody else, instead of his own old record.

'There's a garden for your dog, as well, at my place. He won't get run over there. And a bathroom in the house, so you won't have to cross the yard when you want to piddle, like you do here.'

He'd guessed as much, looking at it from the outside when he'd walked her home but hadn't gone in. It was a bay-windowed house at Hucknall with a gate and some palings along the front.

'It's all settled then, duck?'

'I'll say yes.' It felt like jumping down a well you couldn't see the bottom of. He couldn't understand why he felt so glad at doing it.

She reached across to him. He had such rough strong hands for a man who took all night to make up his mind. Still, as long as there was somebody else to make it up for him there'd be no harm done.

'Every old sock finds an old shoe!' she laughed.

'A damned fine way of putting it!'

'It's what a friend at work said when I told her about us.'

He grunted.

'Cheer up! She was only joking. As far as I'm concerned we're as young as the next lot, and we're as old as we feel. I always feel about twenty, if you want to know the truth. I often think I've not started to live yet.'

He smiled. 'I feel that, as well. Funny, in't it?'

She liked how easy it was to cheer him up, which was something else you couldn't say for every chap.

He polished his black boots by first spreading a dab of Kiwi with finger and rag: front, back, sides and laces; then by plying the stiff-bristled brush till his arms ached, which gave them a dullish black-lead look. He put them on for a final shine, lifting each foot in turn to the chair for a five-minute energetic duffing so that he could see his face in them. You couldn't change a phase of your life without giving your boots an all-round clean; and in any case, his face looked more interesting to him reflected in the leather rather than staring back from the mirror over the fireplace.

A large van arrived at half past eight from the best removal firm in town. She knew how to do things, he'd say that for her. Your breakfast's ready, she would call, but he might not want to get up, and then where would they be? Dig the garden, she'd say, and he'd have no energy. What about getting a job? she'd ask. Me and Raymond's got one, and you're no different to be without. I'm having a bit of a rest, he'd say. I worked thirty years at the pit face before I knocked off. Let others have a turn. I've done my share – till I'm good and ready to get set on again. She was the sort who could buy him a new tie and expect him to wear it whether he liked it or not. Still, he wouldn't be pleased if he took her a bunch of flowers and she complained about the colour. You didn't have to wear flowers, though.

He stood on the doorstep and watched the van come up the street. There was no doubt that it was for him. With thinning hair well parted, and bowler hat held on his forearm, he hoped it would go by, but realised that such a thing at this moment was impossible. He didn't want it to, either, for after a night of thick dreams that he couldn't remember he'd been up since six, packing a suitcase and cardboard boxes with things he didn't want the removal men to break or rip. He'd been as active as a bluebottle that spins crazily to try and stop itself dying after the summer's gone.

When you've moved in with me we'll have a honeymoon, she'd joked. Our room's ready for us, though we'll have to be a bit discreet as far as our Raymond's concerned. They would, as well. He'd only kissed her in fun the other night, but it had knocked Raymond all of a heap for the rest of his short stay there. He'd seen that she was a well-made woman, and that she'd be a treat to sleep with. He hadn't been with anyone since before his mother died, but he felt in need of a change now. I'll have to start living again, he told himself, and the thought made him feel good.

The dog's whole body and all paws touched the slab of the pavement as if for greater security on this weird and insecure morning. 'Now don't *you* start getting on my bleddy nerves,' he said as the van pulled up and the alerted animal ran into the house, then altered its mind and came out again. 'That's the last thing I want.'

He wondered if it would rain. Trust it to rain on a day like this. It didn't look like rain, though wasn't it supposed to be a good sign if it did? What was he doing, going off to live in a woman's house at his age? He didn't know her from Adam, though he'd known people get together in less than the three months they'd known each other. Yet he had never wanted to do anything so much in his life before as what he was doing now, and couldn't stop himself even if he wanted to. It was as if he had woken up from a dream of painful storms, into a day where, whatever the weather, the sun shone and he could breathe again. He smiled at the clouds, and put his hat on.

But if that was so, why had he got a scab on his lip?

He'd been running the gamut of a cold a week ago, and had expected it to be all over by now. Maybe the cold had been operating at his innards even a week before that, and had twisted his senses so much that only it and not his real self was responsible for leading him into this predicament. He was disturbed by the possibility of thinking so. Yet because he wasn't put out by the impending split-up and change he'd rather think it than worry that he'd been taken over by something outside his control. You couldn't have everything, and so had to be grateful for the bit of good to be got out of any situation, whether you'd done it all on your own, or whether it was the work of God or the Devil.

'This is it, George,' the driver called to his mate's ear only a foot away in the cab. 'I'll pull on to the pavement a bit. Less distance then to carry his bits of rammel.'

He heard that remark, but supposed they'd say it about every house unless it was some posh place up Mapperley or West Bridgford. Maybe the dog caught it as well, for it stood stiffly as the cab door banged and they came towards the house.

'Get down, you bleddy ha'porth, or you'll get on my nerves!'

The dog, with the true aerials of its ears, detected the trouble and uncertainty of Albert's soul, something which Albert couldn't acknowledge because it was too much hidden from him at this moment, and would stay so till some days had passed and the peril it represented had gone. The dog's whine, as it stood up with all sensitivities bristling, seemed to be in full contact with what might well have troubled Albert if he'd had the same equipment. Albert knew it was there, though, and realised also that the dog had ferreted it out, as usual, which lent some truth to his forceful assertion that it was already beginning to get on his bleddy nerves.

The dog went one way, then spun the other. All nerves and no breeding, Albert thought, watching the two men stow his belongings in the van. It didn't take long. They didn't even pull their jackets off when they came in for the preliminary survey. It was a vast contraption they'd brought to shift him to Hucknall, and had clearly expected more than two chairs, a table, wardrobe and bed. There'd been more when his mother was alive, but he'd sold the surplus little by little to the junk shop for a bob or two at a time. It was as if he'd broken off bits of himself like brittle toffee and got rid of it till there was only the framework of a midget left. That was it. His dream had been about that last night. He remembered being in a market place, standing on a stage before a crowd of people. He had a metal hammer with which he hit at his fingers and hand till the bits flew, and people on the edge of the crowd leapt around to grab them, stuffing them into their mouths and clamouring for more. This pleased him so much that he continued to hammer at his toes and arms and legs and – finally – his head.

Bloody fine thing to dream about. All his belongings were stowed aboard, but the terrified dog had slid to the back of the gas stove and wouldn't come out. 'You get on my *bleddy* nerves, you do,' he called. 'Come on, come away from there.'

It was dim, and in the glow of a match he saw the shivering flank of the dog pressed against the greasy skirting board. He looked for an old newspaper to lie on, and drag it out, not wanting to get his overcoat grimy. It was damned amazing, the grit that collected once you took your trappings away, not to mention nails coming through the lino that he hadn't noticed before.

'Come on, mate,' the van driver called, 'we've got to get cracking. Another job at eleven.'

There wasn't any newspaper, so he lay in his over-

coat, and spoke to it gently, ignoring the hard bump
of something in his pocket: 'Come on, my old duck,
don't let me down. There's a garden to run in where
you're going. Mutton bones as well, if I know owt.
They'll be as soft as steak! Be a good lad, and don't
get on my nerves at a time like this.'

The men in the van shouted again, but he took no
notice, his eyes squinting at the dim shape of the dog
at the back of the stove. It looked so settled, so finally
fixed, so comfortable that he almost envied it. He
wanted to diminish in size, and crawl in to join it, to
stay there in that homely place for ever. We'd eat
woodlice and blackclocks and the scrapings of stale
grease till we got old together and pegged out, or till
the knockdown gangs broke up the street and we got
buried and killed. Make space for me and let me
come in. I won't get on *your* nerves. I'll lay quiet as a
mouse, and sleep most of the time.

His hand shot out to grab it, as he'd pulled it many
a time through a hedge by the golf course: 'Come
out, you bleddy tike. You get on my nerves!'

A sudden searing rip at his knuckles threw them
back against his chest.

'Leave it, mate,' the man in the doorway laughed.
'You can come back for it. We ain't got all day.'

Standing up in case the dog leapt at his throat, he
banged his head on the gas stove. He belonged in
daylight, on two feet, with blood dripping from his
hand, and a bruise already blotching his forehead.

'Smoke the bogger out,' the driver advised. 'That'll
settle its 'ash.'

He'd thought of it, and considered it, but it would
smoke *him* out as well. Whatever he did to the dog he
did to himself. It seemed to be a problem no one
could solve, him least of all.

'It's obstinate, in't it?' the younger one observed.

'Go on, fume it out,' urged the driver. 'I'd bleddy
kill it if it was mine. I'd bleddy drown it, I would.'

Albert leaned against the opposite wall. 'It ain't yourn, though. It's got a mind of its own.' It was an effort to speak. I'll wring its neck.

'Some bleddy mind,' remarked the driver, cupping his hand to light a cigarette, as if he were still in the open air.

'I can't leave it,' Albert told them.

'What we'll do, mate,' the driver went on, 'is get your stuff to Hucknall, and unload it. You can come on later when you've got your dog out. And if I was you, I'd call in at a chemist's and get summat put on that bite while you're about it. Or else you'll get scabies.'

'Rabies,' his mate said. 'Not fucking scabies.'

'Scabies or rabies or fucking babies, I don't care. But he'd better get summat purronit, I know that fucking much!'

Albert's predicament enraged them more than it did him, and certainly more than the dog. The only consolation came at being glad the dog wasn't doing to them what it was to him. He heard the tailgate slam during their argument, the lynchpins slot in, the cab door bang, and all he owned driven away down the street. There wasn't even a chair to sit on, not a stick, nothing on the walls, nothing, only himself and the dog, and that crumbling decrepit gas stove that she'd said could be left behind because it wasn't worth a light.

He sat on the floor against the opposite wall, feeling sleepy and waiting for the dog to emerge. 'Come on, you daft bogger, show yourself. You get on my nerves, behaving like this.' But there was no hurry. It could stay till it got dark for all he cared. He'd sat out worse things with similar patience. No, it wasn't true that he had, because the ten hours by the body of his mother had passed like half a minute. That was three years ago. He felt as if he had no memory any more. He didn't need one. If everything that had happened seemed as if it had happened only yesterday you didn't need to dwell too much on the past. It didn't do you any good, and in any case it was just as well not to because as you got older, things got worse.

It was daylight, but it felt as if he were sitting in the dark. The dog hadn't stirred. Maybe it was dead, and yet what had it got to die for? He'd fed it and housed it, and now it was playing this dirty trick on him. It didn't want to leave. Well, nobody did, did they? *He* didn't want to leave, and that was a fact, but a time came when you had to. You had to leave or you had to sink into the ground and die. And he didn't want to die. He wanted to live. He knew that, now. He wanted to live with this nice woman who had taken a fancy to him. He felt young again because he wanted to leave. If he'd known earlier that wanting to change your life made you feel young he'd have wanted to leave long before now. Anybody with any sense would, but he hadn't been able to. The time hadn't come, but now it had, the chance to get out of the tunnel he'd been lost in since birth.

But the dog was having none of it. After all he'd done for it – to turn on him like this! Would you credit it? Would you just! You had to be careful what you took in off the street.

'Come on out, you daft bogger!' When it did he'd be half-minded to kick its arse for biting him like that. He wrapped his clean handkerchief around the throbbing wound, spoiling the white linen with the blood. She'd asked if it was faithful when they'd first met in the pub: 'It'll be obedient all right, as long as it's faithful,' she had said. Like hell it was. If you don't come from under that stove I'll turn the gas on. Then we'll see who's boss.

No, I won't, so don't worry, my owd duck. He lay down again near the stove, and extended his leg underneath to try and push it sideways. He felt its ribs against the sole. What a damned fine thing! It whined, and then growled. He drew his boot away, not wanting the trousers of his suit ripped. He sat again by the opposite wall, as if to get a better view of his downfall. The world was coming to an end. It's *my* head I'll put in the gas oven, not the dog's. Be a way to get free of everything.

The idea of shutting all doors and windows, and slowly turning on each brass tap, and lying down never to wake up, enraged him with its meaningless finality. If he died who would regret that he had disappeared? Especially if, as was likely, he and the dog went together. His heart bumped with anger, as if he'd just run half a mile. He wanted to stand up and take the house apart brick by brick and beam by rotten beam, to smash his fist at doors and floors and windows, and fireplaces in which the soot stank now that the furniture had gone.

'I'll kill you!' He leapt to his feet: 'I'll kill yer! I'll spiflicate yer!' – looking for some loose object to hurl at the obstinate dog because it was set on spoiling his plans, rending his desires to shreds. He saw himself here all day, and all night, and all next week, unable to lock the door and leave the dog to starve to death as it deserved.

His hat was placed carefully on the least gritty part of the floor, and he drew his hand back from it on realising that if he put it on he would walk out and leave the dog to die. It's either him or me, he thought, baffled as to why life should be that way. But it was, and he had really pulled back the hand to wipe his wet face, his tears in tune with the insoluble problem.

He leapt to his feet, full of a wild energy, not knowing whether he would smash his toffee head to pieces at the stationary hammer of the stove or flee into the daylight. He spun, almost dancing with rage. Feeling deep into his pocket, he took out something that he hadn't known was there because it had slipped through a hole into the lining. He dropped on to his haunches and hurled it at the dog under the stove with all his strength: 'I'll kill you, you bleeder!'

It missed, and must have hit the skirting board about the dog's head. It ricocheted, shooting back at an angle to the wall near the door. He couldn't believe it, but the dog leapt for it with tremendous force, propelled like a torpedo after the golf ball that he'd unthinkingly slung at it.

Albert, his senses shattered, stood aside for a good view, to find out what was really going on on this mad day. The dog's four paws skidded on the lino as the ball clattered away from the wall and made a line under its belly. Turning nimbly, it chased it across the room in another direction, trying to corner it as if it were a live thing. Its feet again sent the ball rattling out of range.

There'd be no more visits to the golf course tatting for stray balls. The dog didn't know it, but he did, that he'd as like as not be saying goodbye to his tears and getting a job somewhere. After his few dead years without one, he'd be all the better for the continual pull at his legs and muscles. Maybe the dog knew even more than he did, and if it did, there was nothing either of them could do about it.

The dog got the ball gently in its teeth, realising from long experience that it must leave no marks there if the object was to make Albert appreciate its efforts. It came back to him, nudging his legs to show what it had got.

His boot itched to take a running kick at the lousy pest. 'That's the last time you get on my bleddy nerves, and that's straight.'

It was, he thought, the last time I get on my own. It wasn't a case any more of a man and his dog, but of a man and the woman he was going to. He bent down to take the gift of the ball from its mouth, but then stopped as if the shaft of cunning had at last gone into him. No, don't get it out, he told himself. You don't know what antics it'll spring on you if you do. Without the familiar golf ball in its trap the bleddy thing will scoot back to its hide-away. Maybe he'd learned a thing or two. He'd certainly need to be sharper in the situation he was going into than he'd been for the last few years.

He straightened up, and walked to the door. 'Let's get after that van. It's got all our stuff on board.' He raised his voice to its usual pitch: 'Come on, make your bleddy heels crack, or we'll never get anything done.'

With the golf ball still in its mouth there was no telling where it would follow him. To the ends of the earth, he didn't wonder, though the earth had suddenly got small enough for him not to be afraid of it any more, and to follow himself there as well.

The Meeting

She came through from the lounge, passed between two tables in the bar, and asked the waiter to get her a drink.

He noted everything about her: dark hair, pale face, red sweater, big bosom, black slacks and high heels. But there was too much shadow to see more than the barest details of her face.

On her way to sit down he asked her to join him which, to his delight, she did. He offered her a cigarette, and she took it.

'Are you lefthanded?'

'No,' she answered, 'but my father was. Are you?'

'No. My mother was, though. Are you married?'

'Was. We split up.'

'So did I.'

At least he wasn't secretive, which was a good thing, because she knew that secretive men were often rather simple in their relationships with women.

'The best women are divorced,' he said, 'it seems to me.' Every woman responded to flattery, in spite of female enlightenment, or whatever it was called, and he had long since told himself never to forget it.

She laughed. 'And the best men are married.'

'I can tell you don't believe that.'

She sipped her vodka. 'My husband was a spend-thrift.'

'Vodka's best if you knock it back.'

'I know. He'd get through five hundred pounds like a snake on fire.'

He noticed the shifting unharnessed bosom under her sweater when she leaned forward to bring the ashtray close. 'Apart from that,' she added, 'he was a real old sour-socks! You remember that famous picture of 'The Remittance Man Returning From Abroad' with his pathetic expression of wanting revenge yet also needing to be loved? I forget which museum it's in. He looked a bit like that. Very strong minded, in that he never knew what to do. Could only rest and feel wanted when he went into hospital to have his appendix out.'

'Tell me more about him,' he said, also leaning forward. 'You make me sweat.'

'Do I? There's not much to say, though. He was really a greedy little male chauvinist fascist under the skin. We had quite a time. He had that favourite male-swine's trick of pretending to be gentle and good humoured, while I was pushed into being out-spoken and fierce. When we were on our own he was repressive, scornful, and plain bloody mean, just so that he could see my spleen burst when we were in company. The only way I could get my own back was to attack him in front of his friends – all of whom, I suspect, were having the same problems. Either that, or to give *them* a rough time. Then he'd have to soothe them, so that they all thought him a nice, diplomatic, and put-upon sort of person, while I was a shrew. He had a desert in himself, and tried to call it an empire.'

She looked very pleasant to him now. He wanted to asphyxiate himself on her two beautiful plump breasts, give her a kiss on the lips which would hopefully lead to a touch of the tongue, and end in an Epicurean lick of the epiglottis. 'I was happily married for ten years,' he told her, 'so I do have something to be pleased about.'

There was a tremor of curiosity in her deep blue eyes. 'What happened?'

'I came back early one day from my travels – I'm a commercial traveller.'

'So am I,' she put in quickly. 'Hosiery.'

'I'm in electronics. Well, I found her with my best friend. They were eating chocolate-covered wholemeal biscuits with slivers of Cheddar cheese. Both were in the bedroom, with nothing on. She'd been sleeping with him since just after we were married, but I'd had no idea. It had been the talk of the avenue for a long time and everyone thought that as a ménage-à-trois we were supremely happy. If he'd been a stranger I'd probably just told him to clear off, but because he was an acquaintance I half killed him. I threw my wife out as well, then put the 1812 Overture on as loud as possible, till the neighbours had to break the door down and stop it. Then I was all right, and able to get back to work.'

'Do you always smoke a cigar as if it were a haystack?' she asked, when she'd stopped laughing. 'It reminds me of that delectable piece of haddock you usually get for breakfast at this hotel.'

'I like a good smoke.' He finished his whisky. 'A friend of mine drank a bottle of his wife's perfume after a three-day quarrel, and went blind. Nobody ever knew what they had been arguing about, because they led blameless lives, but he didn't get his sight back for a fortnight, and in that time she really went off the rails.'

She made sympathetic noises, unable to get upset

about it. Evenings, after all, were the only times she had to relax. 'A friend of mine had been married to her second husband for two years,' she told him, after a long pause, 'and it suddenly occurred to her that she had never seen him shave. One day she woke up, and he was gone. His appetite, though, had been as regular as sin. She never saw him again.'

He called the waiter over for more drinks. 'Same?'

'All right. I prefer Dutch treat, though.'

'Don't worry, I can afford it. Trade's good. Everybody's got money to buy hi-fis and calculators.'

'They're fun, I know. But I'm making good money, too.'

'It used to be the tobacco that counts: now it's pocket calculators!'

But she didn't laugh, asking instead: 'Do you think it's easier to recognise your own face or your own voice?'

'Know your enemy,' he replied, 'though not *too* well, or you may become like him – or her. Your face, I suppose.'

This seemed to upset her. 'I believe in the voice, really.' It had always been difficult to accept that she had delicate susceptibilities, and as for him – he'd usually preferred to learn the hard way. 'Get me a vodka then, for God's sake,' she said.

He thought she was going to cry, which seemed admissible in a big woman. They always cried sooner than small women.

'I read lately,' she said, making her usual good recovery, 'how common it is for a man and wife to develop the same neuroses as they grow older together. What I think is that they fight each other's neuroses till a benevolent kind of stalemate takes over. This can go on until death. Quite often, though, one or the other can't stand such nullity and takes a lover so as to keep what individuality she's got left. But if it comes back completely it means a divorce.

And then maybe they both begin the whole process again with their new partners – if they're idiotic enough. Maybe such things only happen to weak and ordinary people. But if they do, who does that exclude, I'd like to know?'

'It bloody well excludes me' – though he was sorry he said it so harshly and abruptly. That was the effect she had on him. 'Sex,' he countered, 'becomes too important in a marriage when not enough of it takes place. When the man and woman are so preoccupied with their work that they forget to make love as often as they need, they become antagonistic towards one another without knowing why. They only make love after a quarrel, so it seems that sex is more important than it should be. Or they get to think that the marriage is "based on sex" when it clearly is not.'

She hoped for something better every year, but it was always the same. 'I *did* try to save you.'

He put the expression on his lips that he could never control – simply, of course, because he didn't want to – a mixture of despair and disdain for her and all the world. It was unmistakable, and he always backed up the accompanying deadness of his eyes with some words or other: 'Those who save us destroy us, if we aren't careful to resist their blandishments after we no longer need them.'

With her usual bravado she drank her vodka straight off, which was no more than a cover while she took in his words slowly, so as to get the full cut of their blades. Then she picked up an olive and, carefully putting the stone on the rim of the ashtray, flicked it across the bar and into the lounge. She had picked it so clean with her teeth that it rolled along the well-worn carpet, and tapped against the reception desk – which a dark-haired intelligent-looking woman making enquiries about a room did not notice.

'You never miss,' he said. Her actions had always

been the best part of her, in spite of her throaty voice.

'I work hard,' she said, 'so I have the right to relax in my own way.' He knew all that. By her travelling for a hosiery firm, their tracks crossed often, though each actual meeting had to be deferentially fixed. She was the *chief* traveller, and earned as much as he did.

Now it was his turn to feel like weeping, but he was able to say: 'People like us don't live long enough to see the results of their mistakes. And if they did I suppose they'd only look like glorious moments in an otherwise dull life. Even three hundred years wouldn't be enough.'

She touched his wrist, an indication that, in her view, he was improving.

This made him feel confident enough to add: 'It's a mistake to live in the future all one's life.' He tried to make a last bridge that might bring them together again. 'It's generally pretty miserable, because when you get old you have nothing to live for. Or so my instinct tells me, though I've always believed that instinct to be blind.'

Neither spoke for five minutes, and then she said firmly: 'I know you have. But the first thing you must realise about instinct is that it's not blind, then at least you might be able to get some advantage from it.'

Silence was still their enemy, so he put the usual question: 'What have you been doing with yourself this last year?'

She slurred her words. They were getting drunk. In the room they would, as usual, prove to be no-where near it – but it was necessary for them to feel so in order to get there. 'I don't have much spare time. I know how to look after myself, though. What do you do?'

When their answers to the same questions co-incided he knew they were getting to the end of the evening, though he added earnestly: 'Are you happy?'

She laughed. 'My lip feels dead.'

'Coffee?'

'Please. I read a lot.'

'So do I.' He called for a pot of coffee. It would be as weak as dishwater, merely causing him to get up every hour of the night. He thought it strange how some people never learn. Not to know how to learn showed a fundamental lack of intelligence, even though a person may be very bright and quick on the surface – he suggested.

She poured his coffee. 'Sugar?'

They had made each other suffer, so maybe that alone was love, especially since no marks showed. She used to think he didn't know how to suffer because he suffered too much in silence. If you were in love you'd have the generosity to let the other person see it.

'It seems ridiculous,' he said. 'Yes, I'll have some of that heart-attack white sugar.'

'Don't. I'd hate it if that happened. But what sounds ridiculous?'

'You know what I mean.'

'I don't know what you mean if you don't *tell* me. I don't live in the land of the unspoken any more.'

Everything had to be brought out. They were the ambassadors of two nations, and nothing could be left unsaid. 'Meeting once a year to see if we can't get back together again and make a go of it. That's what's bloody well ridiculous.'

In one way he was right, but at least they'd been able to talk in a civilised way whenever they'd met over the last five years. This hotel was beginning to feel like home. If he threatened to kill himself, or began knocking her about in his quiet far-off tigerish way as if to kill *her*, then at least she would be nearer help than in that detached suburban psycho-box they had lived in. People in that area who thought they'd heard screams would swear it could only have been cats – when it was too late. 'This is the way I like it,' she said firmly.

When they had lived together their love, if such it was, had been one of incurable polarisation. And however tempting it was to return to it she knew that, given her perverse temperament, she must never give in to what she craved. This was the closest she could get to happiness, and she must count herself lucky. She thought it the nearest he could get to it, as well.

His laughter sounded so genuine, and set apart from their insoluble dilemma, that she envied him, though she suspected it, because nothing he had ever done, no sound he had ever made when with her, was not part of some scheme to get at her. 'What are you laughing at?' she asked.

'I once knew someone who put back great quantities of gin, then suddenly stopped drinking on the advice of her doctor. Three months later she died of cancer. She'd been riddled with it. The booze had been holding it at bay.'

'I'll have to think of some good ones for next year,' she said, adding that she would certainly do without *that* kind of drink. He hadn't thought there was much point in it, but he always hoped. 'A score of beginnings,' he said, 'but never an ending in sight.'

If anything would win in the end, she reflected, it was his sense of humour. 'Let's go to bed.'

'I can't tell you how much I'm looking forward to it,' he said.

She was already standing. 'I have to set off for Bristol early in the morning.'

'And I have to go to Hull,' he said, seeing that it was to be the usual thing, after all, but happy at least for the night that was coming.

A Scream of Toys

Edie looked a long time at blue sky in a pool of water after rain before dipping her finger down for a taste.

It got wet. The edge of a cloud was bitter with soil and mouldy brick, telling her that the old backyard was in the sky as well. It was everywhere, even when she walked out and on to the street, and to the road at the end of the street, for wherever she was she knew she had to go back to Albion Yard because that was where she lived.

She liked the water best when it settled into a mirror and showed her face. It wasn't nice to taste the sky, but just to look at the big white cloud creeping back across her frock to cover both knees so that she couldn't see them. You got seven years' bad luck if you broke a mirror, so it was best only to look at it.

She stood up and waved the cloud goodbye, but still saw her mouth and hair saying hello to the sky. It couldn't talk to her, so what was the use? And if it did she'd cheek it back, her mother woud say. She would jump in it except that she didn't want bad luck. If she got any of that her mam would smack her in the chops, and dad would thump her like he did mam when she broke the sugar basin last week.

A horse and cart went along the street loaded with bottles of lemonade that rattled against each other. If one fell she would catch it and run off to drink it dry in the lavatory – but it didn't. The big horse was black and white, and the man on the dray shouted and shot a whip at its neck. If a lemonade bottle did fall it would smash before she could reach out and hold it. It'd be empty, anyway.

She'd like to ride on the horse through the pools of water. It went by in no time, leaving big tods steaming on the cobbles. Mr Jones who worked on the railway opened his door and came out with a dustpan. He scooped 'em up and carried 'em back inside as if they was puddings straight out of the saucepan. She'd like lemonade better, but none fell off. He'd give the puddings to his pot plants for their tea. A woman came out with a broken shovel but she was too late. She would have to wait till she heard another horse and cart, and until Mr Jones was at work, because he always got there first.

When she came back to the puddle it was still there. Nobody had dug it out and taken it away. They didn't like water because there was plenty in the tap, and besides, it was wet. It wasn't so big now though, because the sun had come out.

'You'll come to no good,' she said to herself, playing at her mother, staring at the fire and gazing at the sky. It was wrong to pull your knickers down and pee in water. There'd be no mirror left, but the pool would get bigger, though only for a minute. Johnny Towle put his finger there yesterday and she kicked him on the leg so hard that the buttons flew off her shoe. 'I'll tell yer mam I fucked yer,' he shouted right round the yard. She didn't know what it meant, but it wasn't good, so now she did know.

It was better to look down at the sky when she couldn't see her face.

Next day Johnny Towle came running into the yard, arms wide out, and a big round scream at his mouth, and his eyes shining like the black buttons she had kicked off her shoe.

'There's TOYS,' he shouted to everybody. 'A man's just left a big box of lovely toys at the end o't street. Quick, run, or they'll all be gone.'

'You're daft.' Edie didn't want to run, but her heart shook at his absolute certainty of this abandoned box of real yellow and red treasure-toys waiting for them to dip into and snatch, then take home and play with for ever. Not only his mouth had said it, but his whole body and legs as well, so it must be true, and she ran after the others to get her share.

All it was was a pile of cardboard boxes, and in their disappointment they kicked them to pieces. Johnny Towle booted them harder than anyone, as if he had been tricked as well, but they hated him ever after for his rotten scream of toys when there hadn't been anything but boxes.

When she mentioned it to her mother, her mother said she should have had more bleddy sense because nobody leaves a box of toys at the end of the street. Edie wanted to cry about this, but didn't because maybe one day they would.

When your bones ached you could see a long way off, the tool-setter had once said for a joke, fixing the belt on her machine so that it would go for another half hour at least. Some women were getting new lend-lease machines from America but her turn wouldn't come for at least six months, the gaffer said.

All dressed up and nowhere to go, she stood on Trent Bridge and looked into the water. It was a windy summer so her coat was fastened, causing half the month's toffee ration to bulge from her pocket. The water was like oilcloth. Her bones always ached by Friday night, but she had five bob in her purse, and no work tomorrow or Sunday, so the bit of a backache made her feel better.

When she turned round three army lorries went by and a swaddy whistled at her from the back of the last one. She waved back. Cheeky bleeder. But why not? Amy had asked her to go into a pub but she didn't because you had to be eighteen, though Amy didn't care, for she said: 'We have a sing-song, and it's a lot o' laughs. The Yanks'll always buy you a drink.'

The wind brought a whiff from the glue factory, and the water smelled cold. A barge made an arrow, and a man at the front who steered it wore only a shirt and smoked a pipe, and stared at the bridge he had to go under. She wondered if it would ever come out the other side. If it vanished in the middle and wasn't seen again it would be reported in the *Evening Post*. She wanted to run across the wide road and look over the parapet to make sure. You're not a kid any more, so don't, she told herself, watching smoke come up from its chimney.

She looked at aeroplanes flying over, small black shapes scattered across the sky. Maybe she would go to the Plaza picture-house and see Spencer Tracy or Leslie Howard or Robert Taylor. There might be ice cream on sale. Or she'd call at the beer-off for some lemonade and go home to drink it. If she went in the pub with Amy her mam and dad might be there. Or somebody would see her and tell them. After fifteen planes had gone over she lost count.

A man walked along, and stopped near her. They're going to bomb somebody, but they're brave blokes all the same. Oh dear. He leaned with his back to the bridge, looking at the wide road. He tilted his head at the noise of the aeroplanes, and spoke to himself. She laughed. He didn't like aeroplanes, she thought. His big moustache came over his lips like a bush. If it hadn't been for that he would have reminded her of Robert Donat, who had a thin tash.

She didn't want to look at him in case he thought she was looking at him, and then he would look at her, and she might have to look back, and if you looked at somebody they might not like it. They'd have to lump it, though, so she looked at him anyway. He had dark eyes, and laughed so that his teeth shone. He'll bite me if I don't go away, but it's my bridge as much as his.

The chill wind reminded her that there were ten Park Drives in her pocket. It was so cold she wanted to smoke. Her mam didn't like it so she could never have a puff at home. Her dad smoked, though. His pipe smoked all the time. You'll smoke yourself into a kipper, her mam told him every week when she got his tobacco from the Co-op. So she had to do her smoking at work, one a day in her dinner hour, a packet a week, which left three to spare. At Christmas a woman had given her some rum, and when they got back from the pub she was sick. Then she dropped asleep on a heap of uniforms. The gaffer came by, but didn't say anything. She didn't like boozing after that. The gaffer had had a few, as well.

He was like a soldier, but not quite a soldier, in his greeny sort of uniform. She wanted to walk away, and knew she should, but then he might follow her, so she stayed where she was. The water pushed and shoved itself under the bridge, but she couldn't look at it any more, in case it sucked her in. There was a bit of red and orange in the sky by the War Memorial and paddling pool. A woman walked along the embankment with a pram. The kid in it kicked a shoe off, and Edie heard a smack. Another army lorry came by, but the back was covered up.

The kid cried. She took her fags out, and the man

stared so hard she put them back again. Then he
smiled: 'You walk with me?'

Her grandad had lived with them, and she
wondered why he got smaller and smaller. When he
first came he was bigger than she was, but then he
shrank till he was only a titch, and trembled when he
got up from his chair at night to close the curtains.
When he spilled his tea dad shouted at him. Fancy
shouting like that at your own dad. He used to give
her pennies but then he'd got no money left, so she
gave him one of her fags when nobody was in, but it
made him cough and he threw it on the fire, which
was a waste. When he died he got buried, but mam
and dad didn't wear black clothes at the funeral
because they didn't have any, or couldn't be
bothered, more like. They hadn't been to his grave
since, but she'd gone twice and put wild flowers on,
because you had to visit people's graves after they
died. If you didn't they wouldn't remember you
when you met them again.

It was a daft idea because where would you walk
to when you met each other, but she took out her
cigarette packet and held it towards him. You
couldn't say what he was, because there were no
badges on his battledress that told her anything. He
was funny. He saluted her, then came and took a fag,
looking carefully to choose one, though they were all
the same.

'Thank you,' he said. 'Now, we walk?'

She felt a touch at her elbow, by a hand on its way
to put the fag in his mouth. He puffed while it was
still unlit, waved it about in his lips as she searched
for a box of matches. Her dad bought a lighter at
work which went nearly every time.

'I ain't got any.' She wanted a lighter for herself.
Maybe she would buy one when the war was over,
after she had got a bike and a handbag.

His face was misery, and she was tempted to

104

laugh, till she thought he might not be acting. But he was. His eyes almost closed, and his eyebrows nearly went down to his nose. She had a photo of Robert Donat from *Picturegoer* under her mattress that she took out and looked at with her flashlight before going to sleep. He stretched his arms out wide, smacked his head – even louder than the woman who'd slapped her grizzling kid – undid his top pocket, searched half a minute as if expecting to find a leg of beef there, and fetched a single match out in his fingers. Then his smile was as big as the bridge.

She shivered when he looked at her, and at the lit match between his eyes. 'I'm Italian,' he said, 'prisoner of war – collaborator now.'

He's come a long way, she supposed – watching the lantern made with cupped hands, and then smoke as he put his head almost inside as if he was going to cook it. The dead match somersaulted over the parapet, and she thought she heard a sizzle as it hit the water and was carried away. It'll be in the sea by morning, she didn't wonder.

A man who'd lived next door chucked himself over into the water last year, and drowned. They found the body near Colwick Weir. He'd gone to the doctor's with a sore throat thinking it was cancer, and when the doctor said it was nothing to worry about he thought he was only trying to hide it from him, so did himself in because he'd seen his mother die of it two years ago. There'd been nothing wrong with him at all, except that he'd gone off his head.

He held his cigarette close to hers. 'Now we walk?'

'You'll have to follow me.' She didn't mind at all when he bowed and took her arm. They said at work that foreigners were well brought up, though she supposed everybody was when they wanted something. But when you didn't think you had much to give it was nice to be bowed to like on the pictures, and smiled at, and walked with arm in arm. You didn't care whether it rained or not. And even without being told, he walked on the side the wind was coming from.

Two ATS girls looked at her gone-out. Seen enough, you nosey bleeders? she'd have said if they had stared a second longer. Officers' comforts was what they called them at work, where the two years spent there seemed as long as since she'd been born, a place where she thought she'd learned enough to last the rest of her life.

People couldn't see who you were with when it got dark, so she was glad when it did. Even when walking with Johnny Towle whom she had once gone out with she hadn't wanted to be seen because it hadn't got anything to do with anybody who she was with, and whether she was happy or not, or what they thought she was doing walking out at night.

He'd hardly said a word since leaving the bridge, and now squeezed her arm and walked in step and, as if realising that such silence was no way to behave in face of his good luck at having found someone to talk to him, stopped abruptly and faced her. She was glad when he broke into her thoughts:

'My name is Mario. Your name, please?'

'Edie.'

'Edie,' he said, as if that settled something.

'That's right.'

Mario sounded like a woman's name to her.

'Twenty-eight years,' he said.

'What?'

'Age.'

She'd thought he was at least thirty.

'I'm sixteen,' she told him.

He said he was learning English and asked would she teach him. She said she couldn't teach anybody anything and that if he listened to her his English wouldn't be much good – though because she had sometimes come top of the class at school, she might try.

He said yes please when she stopped at the smell and mentioned buying fish and chips. At the shop you had to get in and shut the door before an air raid warden spotted the light, and Mario had never seen anyone vanish from his sight so quickly.

He leaned against a wall to wait. He almost went to sleep. How to wait was one of the fine arts of a soldier, and he still found it difficult not to regard himself as one. He also knew after eight years in the army that to receive and to have something done for you bound the person to you who gave or did it. There was no surer way. He had money in his wallet which he couldn't share with this pale dark-haired girl.

He had worked in South Africa, and saved it from his meagre pay, yet it was no use to him here. They had been fetched out of camp and put on a train to take ship for England at such short notice that he hadn't had time to change the two big notes for English money. It was true that the camp sergeants had offered to change them, but their rate was so low that he decided to wait and do it later. When they said you couldn't cash them in England he thought they were lying, but after he got here he found it was so.

The fact that he had been robbed never ceased to bite and hurt. It was only one of many such times that something had been taken from him. All through life you were robbed. At the beginning the greatest act of robbery was when you were taken from the safety of your mother's womb and fobbed off with air that barely allowed you to breathe. Nobody had any choice about that, but the various robberies of life multiplied thereafter, each occasion leaving you more at the world's mercy.

Everything contrived to separate you from that

middle area of happiness and dignity. You could never escape the robbery that went on all the time. While you expected to lose watch, shirt, money or boots (having in any case done your share of robbery whenever you'd had the chance, for it was only the poorest of the poor who never got such opportunities) you didn't expect to be parted from your spirit.

He had been brought up to believe that his spirit was of little value, though he'd never accepted the fact. Even so your beliefs were continually waylaid and overwhelmed, but year by year they had become strong again, till such strength was the only thing of importance. As soon as this was realised your spirit got stronger until nothing could break it at last. It had survived the attacks of church and school, and then worst of all the God-almighty State in the shape of Mussolini standing on a shield and held aloft by his gang, the man and the Party you were expected to die for as you had once stood in church and been told to adore somebody who was supposed to have died for you – when nobody had a right to die for you except yourself, and what fool would want to do that? He had had enough for the rest of his life, and smiled at the truth that he would never be able to do anything about such assaults while he continued to blame nobody but himself. Being taken a prisoner of war was the final indignity, but it was also the point from which he had begun to hope.

The fat in the vat was smooth and smoky. The end of your finger would skate if it didn't get scorched. With three people in front she stared at the dark ice starting to split and bubble, and sending up shrouds of lovely mouth-smelling steam when the man poured a wire basket of raw chips in. His scrawny wife who wore glasses and a turban was pulling a handle on spuds that had been peeled white and then fell as neat chips into an enamel bowl.

'Two pennorth o' chips and a couple o' fish, please,' Edie said. She didn't know why she had left Mario outside in the dark, but it wasn't raining so she didn't worry. To be seen with a lad or a man would have made her feel daft, and being with an Italian was as bad as going out with a Yank, she felt, in that people said all sorts of rotten things, and if they didn't say so you could tell what they were thinking, though at work they might have had a bit of a laugh over it. One of the older women could pull a megrim if you as much as mentioned having a good time before peace was declared, in which case somebody was bound to call out: 'Well, Mrs Smith, it's a bleddy free country, ain't it?'

She hoped he'd be gone, but was glad he wasn't.

'Long time.' He hadn't expected to see her again.

She opened the bundle. 'I had to wait till they was done.'

'Done?'

'Cooked.' It was black but the stars were out, and the smell of vinegar and chips drew her face back to the batter-steam and fish clinging to her fingers. 'You'd better get some, or they'll be gone.'

He picked into the paper, and ate more as if to please her than feed any hunger. 'Good.' His approval seemed like a question. 'Thank you.'

Her smile could not be seen in the dark. 'Lovely, aren't they? They don't fry every night, so we was lucky.'

'You are a good girl.' He spoke solemnly, then laughed at her and at himself. The wall held him up. He leaned as if nobody lived inside the house.

He *is* funny, she told herself, though I don't suppose he'll murder me. 'Let's walk for a bit.'

He held her arm in such a way that it seemed to her as if he was blind or badly, and wanted to be led somewhere, 'I was in . . . he began.

'In where?' she asked, after a while.

Their feet clattered the pavement. A soldier passed. Another man in the dark nearly bumped into them, and stood for a moment as if to say something. He smelt drunk. If it was daylight he might have spoken but if so she'd tell him to get dive-bombed, or to mind his own effing business – whichever was more convenient to his style of life – as they said at work, with more laughs than she could muster at the moment. Mario snorted, as if thinking something similar. 'You're in Nottingham now,' she whispered.

'Nottingham, I know.' His normal voice made the name sound like the end of the world, and maybe it was, in the blackout, in the Meadows. 'I was in Addis Ababa. You know where that is?'

'I'm not daft. It's Abyssinia, ain't it?'

He laughed, and pressed her arm. She was glad at getting it right, saw a wild land full of black people and high mountains. Or was it jungle? As they turned into Arkwright Street the crumpled chip paper slipped from her other hand. There was always a smell of soot when it got dark, and a stink of paraffin from factories. A late trolley bus with lights hardly visible was like a tall thin house rumbling along the cobbles. The Methodist Hall was silent, all doors barred against tramps and ghosts.

'It in't a church,' she said. 'It's a British Restaurant. I sometimes eat my dinner there, because it only costs a shilling.'

He seemed to belong to her, even more so when he released her arm and held her hand. At the Midland Station he stopped. 'Not possible to go to centre of city. Not allowed for us.'

She was glad. In Slab Square people would look at them, and talk, and maybe call out. They turned back. She was also angry, because he no longer belonged to her when he couldn't go where he liked. There were different laws for him, so they weren't alone even while walking together in the dark. 'It's daft that we can't go downtown,' she said. 'It's not right.'

He held her hand again, as if to say that he was not blaming her, a warm mauler closing over her fingers. 'Not public houses, either, but cinema we can go.'

Nobody would take any notice if they went and sat on the back row, but it cost more than at the front. Youths would shout out, and there'd be a fight perhaps. 'We can go to the Plaza. That's a nice one.'

He pulled her close into a doorway. He smelt of hair and cloth, and stubbed-out fags – and scent. 'Tomorrow?'

'Don't kiss me, then.'

She couldn't fathom the scent. It wasn't even hair cream. His hair was dry. He didn't, and as they walked along wide Queen's Drive towards Wilford Bridge she shared a bar of chocolate and the bag of caramels from her toffee ration. You had to pay a ha'penny if you wanted to cross the Trent there, so they called it Ha'penny Bridge. To her it always seemed the only real way to get out of Nottingham, to leave home and vanish for ever into a land and life which could never be as bad as the one she'd felt trapped in since birth. But she had only been taken over to play as a child – or she'd gone across for a walk by herself and come back in half an hour because there didn't seem anywhere to go.

They passed the police station, and three years ago she had stood outside reading lists of dead after the air raid, long white sheets of paper covered in typewritten names. Spots of rain had fallen on them, and people queued to see if anybody was on that they didn't already know about.

Houses were heaps of slates, laths and bricks. If anybody was dead a Union Jack was sometimes put over. Johnny Towle's name was on the list. She'd only seen him the Sunday before, when they went to Lenton for a walk. He said he loved her, and sometimes she dreamed about him. A man stopped her when she walked by one smashed house and said: 'Would you believe it? My mother was killed in that house, and I put a flag over it. It ain't there any more. Somebody's stolen it.' He was wild. He was crying, and she told him before hurrying away: 'They'd nick owt, wouldn't they?'

She wanted Mario to talk because she didn't know what else to say after telling everything that had been in her mind, but he wouldn't. He didn't understand when she said: 'A penny for your thoughts!' Everybody must have something in their heads, but he only wanted to walk, and listen to her, asking her now and again to explain a word he didn't know.

Before reaching the bridge she said: 'Let's turn round.' The thought of water frightened her, and she had no intention of crossing to the other side. Their footsteps echoed, and she was glad when she heard others.

'After Abyssinia' – his voice startled her – 'go to South Africa. A long way. Then to England. Soon, Italy, when war is finished. I go to work. War is no good.'

'What will you do?'

'I do business.' He rubbed his fingers so hard that she heard chafing skin before actually looking towards it. '*Affari!*' he said, and she could tell it made him cheerful to say it, the first Italian word she had learned.

'*Affari!*' she echoed him. 'Business!' – so that she also laughed. 'I like that word – *affari.*' She would remember it because it sounded *real*. It was good to do business. Two years ago pennies were short for putting in gas and electric meters, so she and Amy did business by standing on street corners selling five pennies for a sixpenny bit. Some people told them to bogger off, but others were glad to buy. Then a copper sent them away, and she daren't do it again, though Amy did it with somebody else. She used to collect milk money at school so could always get the pennies. Mario laughed when she told him about it.

'*Affari?*' she said.

'Yes, *affari!*'

She knew nothing about him, but liked him because even English wasn't his language, and he had been all over the world. Unlike the lads at work, he was interesting. She took out another cigarette and, embarrassed for him at having to accept it said, hoping he wouldn't be offended: 'Ain't you got any?'

'No. We are paid sixpence a day. Italian collaborators' work. Pay tomorrow, so we go to cinema, both, eh?'

They stood close so as to coax the cigarettes alight. 'You've got a one-track mind,' she said.

'You teach me English!'

On Arkwright Street they turned back towards Trent Bridge. She still wondered whether he was having her on. 'You know it already.'

'I learn. But speech makes practice. Good for *affari!*'

She laughed. He was funny. 'If you like. Pictures, then, tomorrow night?'

'Pictures? Museum?'

She knew it couldn't be hard for him to understand what was said because she'd never been able to talk as if she had swallowed the dictionary. 'No. Pictures means cinema. Same thing.'

She didn't want to lose him, but felt a bit sick after she had agreed. They said at work she never talked, not deep dark Edie Clipston at her sewing and seaming machine earning fifty bob a week. But she did – when nothing else seemed possible. The lad who humped work to and from the machine tried to kiss her, and she threatened him with the scissors, but she let him last Christmas when somebody held mistletoe over them.

'It didn't mean anything, though,' she told Mario as they stood on the bridge. He had a watch, and said it was half past nine. He had to be in by ten, so pressed her hands hard, and kissed one quickly.

He walked away and she forgot all about him. She didn't know what he looked like, and wondered if she would recognise his face on meeting him again. But she felt as if the cobbles had fur on them as she walked back to Muskham Street.

Hearing no noise through the door she tried the knob and was able to go in, glad the house was empty. She filled the kettle and lit the gas. The cat rubbed against her ankle.

'Gerroff, you've had yer supper already.' It followed her around the room, mewing, so she gave it a saucer of bread and milk. Then she put coal on the fire. When they got back from the boozer they might wonder why she'd done so, but she didn't care what they thought.

Her father was tall and thin, and worked on a machine at the gun factory. He took his cap and jacket off and threw them across to the sofa. 'Pour me some tea, duck.'

Her mother came in a few minutes afterwards, pale like Edie but her face thinner and more worn. She took off her brown coat with its fur collar and put it on a hanger behind the stairfoot door. 'What did you bank the fire up for?'

'It's cold.'

'It is when you stand in a queue to buy the coal.'

She sat by the glow to warm her hands. Her legs were mottled already from sitting too close too often. She had never queued for coal, anyway, because a delivery man emptied a hundredweight bag outside the back door every week.

'Kids don't understand.' Her father nodded at the teapot. 'Let's have some, then.'

Joel Clipston had once spent four months in quod for 'causing grievous bodily harm' to a man who, wilting under opinionated hammerblows of logic during an argument on politics had called Joel's wife a foul name as the only way – so he thought – of stopping his gallop and getting back at him. Joel had kept silent in court, ashamed to say out loud what the man had called Ellen, and so he had no defence against having half killed somebody while waiting for opening time outside a pub one Sunday morning. He said nothing to the magistrate, and got sent down for 'such a vicious attack'. There are worse places than Lincoln, he said when he came out, though he was more or less cured of ever doing anything to get sent there again. For a while he roamed the streets looking for the man who had called Ellen a prostitute, but then heard he had gone into the army. If he don't get killed I'll wait for him when he comes out, soldier or not.

He lost his job over the court case, but now that the war had started it was easy to get another. He was set to digging trenches on open ground for people to run into from nearby houses when aeroplanes came over from Germany. If he worked twelve hours a day he made more money than he'd ever had in his pocket before. Then he got work as a mechanic, and found he was good at it. There was either no work at all, or there was too much, but never exactly as much as you needed. He preferred to read newspapers, play draughts, sit listening to the wireless with a mug of tea in his hand, or spend a few hours in the boozer, rather than work more time than he thought necessary – war or not.

They sometimes went over the river at Ha'penny Bridge and into the fields beyond Wilford. In spring Ellen baked lemon curd tarts and made sandwiches, and Joel filled two quart bottles with tea for a picnic by Fairham Brook. The air seemed fresher beyond Wilford village, where the smell of water lingered

115

from the river which rounded it on three sides.

Even though her brother Henry was younger he chased Edie with a stick, till the end of it flicked her, so she turned round and threw it into the river and both of them watched it float away like a boat. Joel was glad they got on so well. Henry was squat-faced and fair, while Edie was dark-haired and had olive skin like her mother.

Edie poured tea into his own big white mug, and put in a whole spoon of sugar. 'When the war's over,' he said, 'I'll get half a ton of sugar from the shop. Then I can put three spoons in. You can't even taste one.'

'Pour me a cup as well, duck,' her mother said. 'Where did you go tonight?'

Edie took the tea-cosy off. 'A walk.'

Her legs ached as well as her back. It seemed a long way that she had gone, though she remembered every place as close enough – but far off all the same when somebody talked to you who had seen so much of the world, and then kissed your hand. The pot was poised over the cup and saucer.

'Where to?' Ellen asked.

'I just went out.' She wondered what else there was to say, for it didn't concern anyone where she had been, and tonight she felt no connection to her mother or father, nor would she to Henry when he came in.

'Sly little bleeder!'

Joel tapped at the bars with a poker. 'You'll never get a straight answer from her.'

It had been the same ever since she was born, that if one of them started to get on at her, the other would always join in. She had the feeling that they knew where she had been, and wanted to drag her out of it and back to what she had always hated. She didn't know how they could tell, but was sure they'd twigged something.

'You ought to stay in at least one night of the week.' Her mother stood up to cut bread for Joel's lunch next day. 'And clean the house up a bit. I have enough to do as it is when I get home from work.'

She had also noticed, as soon as they came in, that both of them smelled of beer. 'I go to work as well,' she reminded her mother, knowing when she spoke that they would have succeeded in pulling her out of her dreams. But she'd never say who she had been with. She brought more than two pounds into the house every week, which seemed enough for them to get out of her. 'I scrubbed the parlour floor last Sunday, didn't I?'

Hot tea sprayed over the saucer and the cloth, and the pot rolled itself on to the floor before she could stop it. The cup broke with the weight of the big brown teapot. She didn't know how. Dropped on to it. The noise shocked every bone, and she stood with fingers curled as if the pot were still gripped – or as if, should she keep them held like that, the teapot bits would reassemble and jump back into place.

In spite of her mother saying that she was always in a dream, that she was as daft as they come, that she had never known anybody to be so clumsy – and several other remarks that she wouldn't listen to but that would come back to her later when, she knew, she would have even less use for them – she felt that if there had been a hammer close enough she would have lifted it and smashed the remains of the teapot and cup to smithereens.

But she didn't care as she looked at the bits of pot mixed among the tea leaves and stains. She remembered Mario's face by the bridge, when he had taken the cigarette and put a hand over while lighting it, as close as if the whole meeting was happening bit by bit again. She saw both herself and him as real and plain as ever, the pair of them right by her side. The picture hypnotised her, and held her rigid with surprise and a feeling that gave some protection for what was sure to come now that she had smashed the teapot.

'She allus was clumsy,' her father put in, a mild response which told her to be on her guard. The jollier they were on coming home from the pub only meant that they would be even more nasty and hateful later. It was best to be out of their way at such times, but unless you went to bed there was nowhere to take refuge, and she didn't want to go to sleep so early after talking to Mario.

'I couldn't help it.' She heard the tone of fear, apology and shame, which made her more angry with herself than at dropping the teapot. The accident didn't seem important, anyway. She wasn't a bit clumsy at work. 'My fingers slipped.'

Her father put his half drunk mug of tea on the mantelshelf, as if it would be safe from her there. 'What am I going to do in the morning, then? There's nowt to make the tea in.'

If she looked up he would hit her, but in turning away she saw his grey eyes lifeless with anger, and his lips tight. Ellen picked a few bits of the saucer from the cloth.

'Let *her* do it,' Joel said quietly. 'She dropped the bleddy thing.'

He sometimes chased her and Henry around the room in fun. All three laughed, but Ellen looked on as if thinking they should act their age and have more sense. But the last time Joel had been playful they suddenly felt too old for it. The time had passed when they could play together.

Edie sometimes said things without thinking, and when she did she was frightened. If she had known beforehand that she was going to be frightened she would still have spoken because she was never able to stop herself even when she thought about it. The words seemed to jump from outside of her: 'I'm not going to clear it up.'

He sat down with his tea, and she felt sorry she had cheeked him, so picked some brown sharp pieces of the teapot to put in a little heap on the corner of the table. This methodical enjoyment of her task caused a flash of rage to blot out Joel's brain. Edie knew it was only right that she should try to clear the mess up, though her mother had already done most of it, and had come back from the coal place with a dustpan to start clattering bits on to it.

It couldn't have been worse if a ten-ton bomb had dropped on the place and killed them. All because of a teapot, Edie told herself, about to cry, as if she alone in her might and viciousness had broken the spirit of the house. There was such gloom that, after a few moments, the only thing possible was to laugh. She wanted to be walking again with Mario – while doubting that she ever would – crossing a bright green field with him, under a pale blue sky full of sunshine instead of bombers.

It was as if her father had picked up the wall and hit the side of her face with it. She wondered how he knew what she had been thinking. The blow threw her across the room, and coconut matting scraped her skin as she slid with eyes closed and banged her head at the skirting board. In darkness she saw nothing, but it was followed by a dazzle of blue lights as his boot came at her.

When her father lashed out like this her mother always got on at him to have more sense, and now she tried to pull him off, telling him not to be stupid or he'd get in trouble knocking her about like that, thinking of the times he'd pasted her, Edie supposed, but then wondering if she interfered out of spite, because he only answered by giving her another kick that was worse than the rest.

As she lay half stunned Edie knew she would go to

the bridge again and meet him as often as she liked
because he had been so gentle and interesting. They
didn't know, but even if they did they couldn't stop
her seeing somebody who made her feel she need
never be anybody except herself.

After a parting half hearted kick at her back which
she hardly felt, her father sat down to light his pipe
and finish his tea, ignoring her agonised and shouted
out wish that it would choke him.

The drawn curtains in her room made the blackout
complete, but when she put off the light it was so dark
she couldn't go to sleep. She ached from the last big
kick but cried no more, not even when she hoped a
German plane would drop a single bomb on them
and make the blackout so final that they would never
be able to switch a light on again.

She'd die of shame if daylight ever came, but if it
did, she would never let anybody hit her again. If her
father lost his temper and tried to, she would blind
him with whatever she could grab. That sort of thing
was finished from now on. She didn't know how, yet
knew it was, because she had made up her mind,
hoping that when it looked like happening she
would be able to remember what she had made up
her mind to do, and blind him no matter what.

She heard them arguing downstairs, though not
what was said. Their speech sounded like the flood
of a river hitting a bridge before going underneath.
Now that she wasn't there they could start on each
other. They could kill each other for all she cared.
They had been cat-and-dogging it for as long as she
could remember, but no wonder when she thought
about what her mother used to get up to.

When dad was out of work – she would tell Mario
(whether he could understand or not, because if you
didn't tell your thoughts to somebody there was no
point in living) which went on for years and years –

mam kept going downtown at night saying she was off to Aunt Joan's, but one day after she'd bought some new shoes and a coat, and things for the house as well, and wouldn't say where she had got the money, dad followed and saw her on Long Row talking to somebody in a car.

He felt so rotten at the idea of her picking up men that he hadn't got the guts to put a stop to it. He didn't even let on he knew, though she must have known he did. But one night, after it had gone on for a long time, he decided he'd had enough, and caught her sitting in Yates's Wine Lodge as large as life with a man who'd had his nose blown off in the last war. Where the nose should have been there was wrinkled skin and two small holes that dripped if he didn't press a hanky to it.

When dad saw this he let his fists fall, but swore at them both and told mam never to come home again or he would murder her and the kids and then cut his own throat. Me and Henry liked what happened, because dad didn't even shout at us now she wasn't there. He pawned her clothes one day, and took us on a trackless into town and treated us to the pictures and an ice cream each with the money. The woman who lived next door often gave us toffees when we came home from school because she was sorry for us having no mother. It made us feel like orphans, and we liked that.

We were drinking tea and eating toast one night when somebody knocked at the door. The tap on wood was soft, as if a beggar was hoping we'd ask him in and give him some of our supper, and when dad opened it we were surprised to see old No-nose come in from the cold. Dad was mad at being disturbed from his newspaper and his peace, but No-nose asked: 'I want to know if you'll be kind and take your Ellen back.'

'Take bloody *who* back?'

'Your Ellen,' No-nose said.

Dad stood by the mantelpiece, as if ready to crank his arm up for a real good punch. No-nose stayed just in the door. He wore a nicky-hat and was wrapped up in a good topcoat and scarf – as well as gloves – because he had an office job and was better off than us. He would have been goodlooking if he'd still had a nose.

Me and Henry was too frightened to say anything, and when dad, after a bit of an argument in which nobody said much, said that mam could come back if she liked, No-nose looked as happy as if his nose had come back on to his face, which made us want to laugh – though we daren't in case dad turned on us.

He went out to get mam. She'd been standing at the end of the street waiting for him to come and tell her whether it was all right or not. No-nose gave us some chocolates and sixpence each, then went away after shaking dad's hand but saying not a word to mam. He only nodded at her, as if he'd had enough of the trouble she'd caused – though he was to blame as well.

When he'd gone mam sat on the other side of the fireplace to dad. They scowled at each other for half an hour. Then mam laughed, and dad said a string of foul words. He's going to get the chopper and kill her, I thought, but suddenly he was laughing and so was she. Me and Henry was even more frightened at that, and said nothing, because we weren't able to make things out at all.

Mam and dad kissed, and sent us to buy a parcel of fish and chips out of the few quid that No-nose had given her. Afterwards we had a good supper, and everybody was supposed to be happy, though I wondered how long it would last.

When Edie started to feel more sorry for them than for herself she fell asleep.

With her coat tight-wrapped around her, and holding Mario's two South African banknotes folded into her pocket, Edie went downtown into Gamston's Travel Agency to try and change them for him. She was glad that only one other person was being served as she opened the notes out and showed them over the counter, feeling daft because she had not been in the place before.

'Can't change 'em,' the bloke said, an old man with a moustache who first looked over his glasses at them and then at her.

'Why can't you?' Money was money, she'd always thought, and Mario had earned every penny of whatever it was called.

He held a pen, as if about to write all over her face. 'Because we can't. We're not allowed to, that's why.'

She stood, hoping he'd alter his mind, whether they were supposed to or not. 'Oh.'

'We can't, anyway. It's regulations.'

He went to get a railway ticket for somebody but, not wanting to leave without doing what she had come for, she didn't move. Last night Mario had showed her some photographs of his mother and sister, and his two brothers, and they all looked as nice as Mario himself, and she felt that if she couldn't get his cash changed she'd be letting them down as well as him. So she held up the large gaudy-coloured banknotes again.

The man came back. 'There's nothing I can do for you. It's foreign money, and there's a war on, and that's why we can't change it. Come in after the war, then it might be all right!'

'It'll be too late then. I need it now.'

A woman behind the counter put a cup of tea by his elbow, and maybe he didn't want to let it get cold because he said, as if ready to fetch the police to her: 'Where did you get 'em from?'

She saw by his face, and knew from his tone, that

he thought she had nicked them or – she screwed the words painfully into her mind – earned them like *that*. Her mouth filled with swearing, but she couldn't spit it at him as he deserved, so walked out and then went quickly along Parliament Street towards a café where she could get a cup of tea.

The sun was in her eyes so she turned her back to it. When Mario walked on to the bridge she gave him the banknotes: 'Sorry.'

'No *affari*?'

'The bleeders wouldn't do it.'

He scowled. 'Bleeders?'

She explained.

'Never mind.'

Neither spoke for half an hour. They walked by rowing boats tied to wooden landing stages, and she wondered when and at what place they would reach the sea if she and Mario got into one of them. Maybe they'd land on a beach in Italy, and have no more trouble from anybody.

He held her hand tightly, so she knew he was brooding about something which it was no use asking him to explain. But he didn't seem angry. He was miles away, living in sounds and colours she had no hope of understanding, though she liked the warm and dreamy feeling when she tried to picture them. With an English bloke she wouldn't have had such dreams. They'd have joshed and teased like kids – whereas with Mario she saw mountains and yellow trees, and a sky so blue it would blind you if you looked straight at it. But she didn't want to because her dream was too far beyond her normal mind. You had to be grateful for small mercies, and this was bigger than most.

Grey water slopped at the concrete steps. There was a noise of children playing from the other side of the river. She felt easy with him because, though he had suffered and was far from home, he had a light heart and could make her laugh. But she took his larger hand in order to share his bitterness, and let whatever he felt was too much to bear pass into her. She had always known that there were some things you could only keep quiet about, though realised now that the one way of filling such silence was by touch.

The streak of green and blue turned into the last flush of the day. Children stopped playing suddenly. They were alone on the embankment with no one to see them. Not that she cared. She'd hold his hand whoever was looking on. They could take a running jump at themselves for all she'd bother. Once upon a time she had clutched her father's hand, but she hadn't spoken to that bully for days.

'Never mind,' she said to Mario. 'They're dirty robbers, that's what they are.'

Her whole body shook when he kissed her, and she could never remember feeling so protected.

'I love you,' he said.

She didn't know how to say anything. To speak like that seemed a funny way of putting it, though. They walked on, and she couldn't find words to answer, even when he said it again. It was time to say goodnight, and promise to meet another day, but she couldn't stop walking and say anything while still so close to that total change already made between leaving home and meeting him. To walk away from the comfort of holding hands seemed neither right nor possible.

She still felt stupid at not having got some English money for his foreign banknotes, but it was a failure that brought them closer, and made her want to stay longer with him, so that she was almost glad they'd been so rotten to her at the travel agent's.

A policeman stood talking to the woman tollkeeper who leaned by a tiny brick house to collect money from any carts or motors that went over Ha'penny Bridge.

'Not go there,' Mario said.

There was plenty of dusk to hide in, so she wondered what he meant. They were on the lowest step by the water which, had it come up another inch, would have flowed over her shoes. 'It don't matter, does it?'

'In camp at ten. No Italian out after ten o'clock.'

It was too late, anyway. The world was full of trouble when you did things that caused no harm. She wondered who started it, but didn't know. If Mario walked about after ten at night it wouldn't stop the day beginning tomorrow. 'Will you get shouted at?'

He smiled. 'I have given sergeant money. But the police don't know, and they ask for papers, maybe, then send me back, and tell Captain. Then Mario will not walk with Edie for three weeks.'

If they crossed Ha'penny bridge to the fields they'd be safe from prying eyes – and from having to make up their minds to go anywhere. He pressed his face to her hair, and said things she didn't understand but that she was happy to hear. She was also glad she had washed her hair last night.

He led her up the steps and back to the roadway. 'Police gone now,' he whispered.

She took two ha'pennies from her pocket. The old woman at the gate wore a thick coat and scarf to keep out the damp. The river pushed itself forcefully along, and the other side seemed far off from where they stood. The noise of a cow sounded from the fields.

The tollkeeper took her ha'pennies. 'You'd better be back before twelve.'

'Are you going to wind up the bridge, then?' Edie asked, thinking that coming back was too far in the future to worry about.

'Cheeky young devil!' the old woman called.

A sliver of sharp moon showed as if about to come down and cut the river to ribbons. But there were streaks of night mist towards Beeston, and white stars glittered above. Halfway over, Mario said: 'You give her money?'

'Only a penny. It's a *toll* bridge.'

'Toll?'

'Money to pay,' she said. 'Somebody private owns it.'

He walked more quickly. 'Not good.'

'It's always been like that.'

Her arm was folded with his so she had to keep pace. A plane flew over. 'One crashed last year. An American plane. The pilot knew a woman in a house at Wilford. He went over ever so low to wave at her. But he crashed, and everybody in the plane was killed.'

She didn't know whether he understood. It didn't seem to matter, but she went on: 'Five men died, and all for nothing. The pilot had wanted to say hello to his girl. And now she will wear black for evermore because he is dead. And she had a baby afterwards and they couldn't get married. She saw his plane blow up when it hit a tree with no leaves on in the middle of a field.'

'Bad story,' he said.

At the end of the bridge they walked down the lane, no lights showing from any house. They were used to the dark. She didn't know on which field the plane had crashed, but perhaps it was near Fairham Brook where she used to play with Henry when they went on picnics from Albion Yard. At work they'd said what a shame it was, and wondered whether the poor girl would ever get over it, and what would happen to her baby if she didn't, because she was packed off to live with her grandmother in Huntingdonshire. Others heard she'd killed herself, but all sorts of rumours flew about, and you couldn't believe anything, though she wouldn't be surprised.

When he stopped singing it was only to kiss her hand. She heard the grating cry of a crow from the river that looped on three sides of them. She liked his tune, and would have sung a bit herself if she had known it, though she was happy enough to listen as they went through the village that seemed dead to the world and into a field where they would stay till the bombers came home.

Confrontation

'When I last saw you – a year ago,' Mavis said resentfully, and with more disappointment than he cared to notice, 'you told me you had only three months left to live.'

He remembered it vividly, while reflecting that mendacity was an illness for which there was no proper cure. It was possible to recover from it, however, when you had no more need of such unsubtle ruses. In other words you might grow out of lying by the simple process of growing up. He hoped it was only a matter of time, that though old habits never die they might simply fade away.

It happened at June and Adrian's party, a disaster that was indeed difficult to forget. What's more, his ploy hadn't worked, so he might just as well have saved himself the trouble of lying. Yet it *was* undeniable that he had lied, and enjoyed it. He could only apologise to her – first, because he was still here on earth to make her remind him of it; and second, that he was still alive and might yet lie again.

His apology didn't seem to make much difference.

Her disapproval was so profound that he saw some chance of them getting to know each other better. She watched him take a cigarette out of his packet, then put it back. He wasn't going to lie again, after all. Or perhaps it only meant he wasn't going to smoke much today. He was showing her that he was cutting down his smoke production, so that at least he couldn't convincingly repeat his lie of a year ago.

'I've only got three months to live,' he had said.

She laughed, loud. 'You're joking.'

The folds of her red-and-white African safari-wrap shifted under her laughter. She was big and fair and, talking to someone a few minutes ago, he'd heard that she had just left her husband. He thought he couldn't go wrong, until he told his silly lie.

'Well, no, I'm not lying, or joking, though it sounds stupid, I admit. I wish to God I was. It was only this afternoon that I was told.' He looked straight into her face, and watched the expression change. If you weren't merciless to people who made fools of themselves they would never believe in you again.

Her features showed an inner horror, as if she had touched previously unfathomed depths of callousness in herself – which frightened her far more than any predicament he might be in at having only three months left to live.

'I'm sorry,' he said, 'really I am. I shouldn't have told you. You're the first one. Why should I burden you with it? Even my wife doesn't know yet. I only heard today, in any case, and I haven't been home. I went to see a blue movie in Soho, then came straight on to June and Adrian's shindig.'

They stood in the small garden, in which only a few others had sought refuge from the crushing noise because most people thought it was still too damp outside. 'Are you here because you know

June – or are you a friend of Adrian's?' he asked, in what he hoped would be construed as a valiant attempt to change the subject.

It was his faint northern accent that brought back the feeling that he might still be lying. The only thing that stopped her disbelief was the fact that no one in the world would lie about such a matter. 'Both,' she told him.

'I don't even believe it myself,' he said, 'so if you think I'm lying I can easily understand.'

Maybe so few people came into the garden, he thought, because it was close to the main road, and a huge bar of orange sodium light glowing above the hedge had the ability to plunge its searching fire into any heart, and detect those untruths which everyone used at times like these. But against a *monstrous* lie it would have no power.

She felt herself unfairly singled out to receive this terrible information. It was as if someone had come up and married her without her permission. Her soul had been sold in some under-the-counter slave-market. At the same time she felt privileged to be the first one told – though a gnawing uncertainty remained.

'Forget it,' he said. 'I shouldn't have spoken. I feel slightly ridiculous.'

Her husband had never told her anything. If he'd heard from his doctor that he was going to die he'd have kept the information to himself and slipped out of the world without a murmur, so that she'd be left with the plague of having nagged him to death. Her frequent and fervent cry had been: 'Why don't you *say* something? Speak, for God's sake!' Once when they got into bed, after a day of few words passing between them, she said in a friendly tone: 'Tell me a story, Ben!' He didn't even say goodnight by way of reply. Thank heavens all *that* was finished.

She touched his wrist. 'It's all right. It's better to

speak.' The glass she held was empty. In the glow of the sodium light it was difficult to tell whether he was pale or not. Everyone looked ghastly under it, and she understood why most of the others stayed inside. Adrian and June must have bought the house in summer, when the days were long.

'It's not,' he said, 'but I'm one of those people who can't really help myself. If I'm not talking I'm not alive. I often wonder if I talk in my sleep.'

Illness that is fatal, she had read, was nearly always brought on because the inner spirit of the afflicted person was being prevented from opening and flowering – or simply from a lack of the ability to talk about yourself and your problems. He didn't seem to be stricken in that way at all, though every rule had its exceptions – so they say.

'I've often thought of buying one of those ultra-sensitive modern Japanese tape-recorders which are switched on by the sound of your own voice,' he said, 'then playing it back in the morning to see if I've uttered any profundities, banalities, obscenities, or just plain baby-talk during the night.'

Her husband, who had been in advertising, had believed so much in the power of the spoken word that he would say very little, except perhaps at work, where it could be taken down and transcribed by his secretary, and used to make money. She dredged around at the back of her mind for something to say. Maybe her husband had been right when, in reply to one of her stinging accusations that he never said anything, rapped back: 'It takes two to make a silence.'

'But I never did,' he laughed. 'They're too expensive. Anyway, I might have said something that would have frightened me to death! You never know. And in any case, when I say something I like to make up my mind about what I'm going to say a second or two beforehand.'

'Is that what you're doing now?'

People were coming out through the open french windows with plates of food. Neither the sodium lights nor the damp would bother them if they had something to do, such as eat.

'Absolutely,' he told her, 'but because I'm talking to *you* I don't let it stop me.'

The northern accent, slight as it was, far from making him seem untrustworthy, now had something comforting about it. If he'd had the accent, and spoken very little, it would have been merely comic. But he had something to say, and that was different. He was also using it to good effect, she suspected.

'What work do you do?' It wasn't much to ask, but it was better than nothing.

He named one of the minor publishing houses, that was trying to become a big publishing house but was having a hard time of it. 'I work for them, but I'll be giving it up. *Force majeure.*'

'Perhaps things aren't as bad as you think.'

'The same thought crosses my mind – every alternate minute.' He suddenly got tired of it, and thought that if he didn't go and talk to somebody else he really would be dead in three months – or even in three seconds – from boredom. 'I must have a drink,' he said, glancing down. 'Be back soon.'

Later she saw him from a distance, talking intently to someone else. He came behind her in the queue for food, turned round because he had forgotten to pick up his napkin-roll of knife and fork, and looked at her as if she were a mirror. Thank God she'd stopped herself in time from smiling and saying something. After heaping up his plate with a choice of everything he walked over and talked to a woman with grey hair, an iron face, and a big bust.

She observed him for a while, convinced he wasn't spinning the same tragic tale he'd put out to her – though not doubting that it was something with an equal come-on bite. He wore a formal and finely cut navy blue suit, had black hair and dark eyes, which did make him look even more pallid under the light inside the house.

She asked someone who he was, and he said: 'Oh, that's Tom Barmen' – as if even talking to him was a peril no level-headed person got into, so she went upstairs to where June and Adrian kept the telephone directories, and found that he lived on Muswell Road, which wasn't far away. She dialled the number, and a woman's voice answered. 'Is that Mrs Barmen? I'm afraid I have rather sad news for you.' Someone had to tell her, after all.

'Would you rather be a man or a woman?' Joy Edwards asked, when Mavis got to the bottom of the stairs.

'Depends for how long,' she said.

'All day,' Harry Silk laughed, muscles bulging under his sweatshirt, a hand flattened on his bald head.

'Five minutes,' said his wife, heavily pregnant.

This was more like a party, Mavis thought, saying: 'Both at once? Or one at a time?' – and went to the bar for another glass of white wine, not caring now whether she got tight or not. She'd said all she had to say, for one evening at least.

When the doorbell rang, sounding faintly above the noise, she thought it was a taxi come to collect someone. Because it was after midnight one or two people had already left. A tall woman, still with her coat on, pushed through the crowd. By the kitchen door there was a crash of (unfilled) coffee cups, though the woman who had just arrived was not the cause.

'It's Phyllis Barmen,' she heard someone say.

She met him a year later at a publisher's cocktail

party in the huge new Douglas Hotel. In the crowd
she saw a hand throw down the end of a cigarette so
that it went into a tray of peanuts instead of the
ashtray. She looked up and saw who it was. He was
dressed in the same suit, or one very similar.

'Did I?' he said, in response to her accusation. 'I'm
sorry about that. Parties are so deadly boring.'

'The end of the last one, where we met, was quite
exciting – I thought,' she reminded him.

'Thanks to you.' He looked as if he wished that *she*
had only three months to live – or less.

'I suppose we should both apologise, really.'

She was totally miscast in her assumptions, he said
to himself. Her mind was misshapen, the whole
bloody lot warped.

She sensed she was misreading everything,
judging from his mischievous look. It was devilish.
She was glad there were other people around them.

'You were chosen,' he said. 'I knew I could rely on
you, though you were so long going to the telephone
that I was beginning to wonder whether I'd made a
mistake. But when I saw you go up the stairs I knew
I'd picked a winner.'

He had taken her seriously, at least.

She had taken *him* seriously, which wasn't bad
going.

'I needed one more public set-to with my wife to
end my deadly boring marriage,' he said. 'She
wanted it too, so never feel guilty about it. It was
quite mutual. We're well shut of each other now. I
did feel sorry for June and Adrian, mind you.'

'So did I.'

'But they couldn't say they were bored for that last
half hour. I haven't seen them since, though.'

'They miss you.'

'I'm sure they do.'

She couldn't resist gloating. 'All this is pure hindsight on your part.'

'There's no such thing as hindsight – in my way of looking at things.'

'You didn't plan it at all,' she persisted.

She felt so kicked in the stomach that when he asked her to go out to dinner after the party she said yes, and from that time on never had a moment to wonder whether she had done the right thing or not. It became more and more obvious, however, that she had been just as scheming when she'd gone upstairs to make the telephone call at June and Adrian's party, and over the years it was easy enough to make sure that he knew it.

Ear to the Ground

Bleeders. They don't know they're born. Never done a day's work in their lives. Don't expect to, that's the trouble. They don't tell 'em at school that one day they'll have to go out into the world and earn a living. Schools aren't like that any more: all play and no work. If the teacher tells 'em off they get up and thump him. They sort him out. One teacher was a walking vegetable afterwards, and they had to fetch the police.

Not like when I was at school. Knocked me silly once when I blotted my arithmetic book. It wasn't anything, really. Hadn't done a wrong thing at all. The teacher just come up and pulled me to my feet, and started bashing. Saw stars, I did. Didn't know what he was on about. I was only ten. If the bleeder would try it now I'd kill him.

These days, though, the kids rule the roost at school. Then they go home and see what their fathers have brought in from work, or what they've stolen, rather, or what's fell off the back of a lorry. Or they sit round the fire and laugh at his tales about skiving

137

and all the things he got away with behind the foreman's back. Or they don't even go to work. Pay a penny a week off the arrears of the council rent and get all the supplementary benefits they can lay their hands on. Rob-dogs, that's what they are.

Send their kids out skiving while *they* sit at home in bone-idleness. Daughters go on the streets. Some stay there. The sons go out to nick cars. Drive straight up the motorway to sell 'em in Glasgow, then come back first class on the train with their pockets full of money. Coppers waiting on the station, often as not. After a while they come up in court. And then what happens? Get let off. Probation. No proof. Talk themselves out of anything. Maybe they even slip the copper a tenner or two. Who am I to know what goes on? And if they do get sent to Borstal they can relax because they don't have 'em to keep for a couple of years. The parents don't want 'em. They're all the same. What a life they lead! Living off the fat of the land. National Health. National Insurance. National Assistance. National *Insistence*. Sickness Benefit. Family Allowance. Extra-that. Supplementary-this. Index-linked dole. You name it, they get it. Generation after generation in the same family.

Nobody works any more. Best if some of 'em don't, if you ask me. Safer when they're not at work. Better for the others. Less trouble having 'em on the dole. Why should they work, anyway? There's money for the asking. Spend it all in the bookies', though, betting on hosses. Boozing in the pubs. I don't know – but I know they do. I ain't read about it. I've *seen* it. Gone on for years. Not your bleeding Blackies, either, mate. Some on 'em are, but it's whites, mostly. Country's rotten. And why? I don't know. No religion, I expect.

We aren't all like that, though. Bloody good job, ain't it? I'm not, anyway. Would be if I didn't make an effort. Look at me. Go on, look at me, then: twenty years at the same firm, and then they went bust. Van driver, I was. Well, they went broke after I left, but they got rid of me in good time, I will say that for 'em. Just because one of my so-called colleagues in the van driving industry said I'd lifted summat off the back of a wagon that didn't belong to me. Sacked me straight off, without giving me the chance to explain. Talk about injustice. You can say goodbye to that, these days. There's none left. Not for a bloke like me, anyway.

I'd given my unstinted loyalty for twenty years, sweated all the time because I wanted a steady job after leaving the army. An ex-swaddy, an old soldier who's done his two-year call-up for his country, but a blind bit of difference it made. Nobody respects it. People think it's nothing. Your kids laugh at you when you tell 'em you was in the army. But I served my bloody country, I did, all the same. And a lot of good it gets you.

So I've been on the dole for six months because there was no work for me. Plenty of labouring, washing-up jobs, sweeping the streets – stuff like that. What did they take *me* for? A tramp? There's a million out o' work, I said. Save it for them. Give it to the school leavers. But not me, mate. Stuff it. What do you think I am? I'm a fully qualified van driver of long experience.

And they wanted me to go on a building site! Go and get dive-bombed, I said. Cheeky bleeders. Me, a van driver *collecting dustbins*. They'd stamp you into the ground. *Carrying bricks!* So I stayed on the dole. I've worked twenty years, paying your rotten stamps, I told the four-eyed bleeder at the labour exchange, as well as income tax, so now *you* keep me. I want a bit of it back. What have I been paying it for all these years? Well, go on, tell me, then. *You* tell *me*. Why? To keep you bleeding penpushers sitting on your arses? Not bleeding likely. I'm a *van driver*, mate, not a *roadsweeper*. So you can stuff your jobs, and get me a proper one. *Washing up in a canteen!* Is that a man's job? Oh, I know, you've got plenty of work, no end of vacancies, but it's a *job* I want, mate, not work. Not that sort of work, any road up.

I've got kids to keep – three kids at school still, going out every day at a quarter to nine. Coming back at half past four. And they do that, day after day, and year after year. Do you know what they learn? Do you? You think you do, but you don't. I know I've told you already, but I'm telling you again. You won't believe me, tosh. *Nothing*. That's what they learn. They learn nothing. Oh yes, they learn to read and write – but that's about it. Some of 'em do, anyway. Any dim bleeder can do that. They don't learn about life, though, and how to work. And respect for their parents. They don't respect *me* – not me who has worked his arms and legs off for twenty years. No, not on your fat gut, they don't.

They'd respect me if I was a layabout, though, wouldn't they? If I was a scrounger and a shirker they would. The world loves a skiver. *My* kids would. I'm telling you they would – if I lived like some of the bleeders lived, sponging all their lives off the system and sending their kids out for what they could get, and giving their wives the wink to do a bit of you-know-what on the sly to pay the gas bill. Up to all sorts of tricks. Born to it. You might think so, anyway, they do so well at it. But they are – they're born to it in this country, that's why.

But I'm not like that. I look after my kids. Yet they don't respect me for it. They bloody don't. They come home, the little bleeders, and eat all they can lay their hands on, then ask me for money to go out and spend. They don't even tell me what they'd spend it on if I had it to give 'em. Toys and chips and toffees, I expect. And do you know what my fourteen year old lad had the cheek to say when I said I'd only enough money left for fags till his mother got the Supplementary Benefit on Monday? He said: 'If we ain't got any money then, why don't you go and get a job like Mr Thompson next door did last week? Then we'd have some money, wouldn't we?'

As large as life he said it. I swear to God he did – shoving his pimply face and scruffy puffed-up hair at me, as if he could say anything now that he was nearly my size. I grabbed him by the plastic jacket covered in badges. Where'd he got that jacket? His mam hadn't bought it for him. The cheeky bleeder, to tell me off like that. I'll kill him, I thought. My old man would. Killed me, the bastard. He would, an' all. All fist and spit.

I landed him the biggest bloody clout I'd given him for a month, so he got summat free, anyway! I said if he wanted money he could go about getting it himself. He'd get no more from me. Not another penny, I shouted at him. I'm not keeping you till you're sixteen. I left school at *fifteen*, I did. Go out and see if it grows on trees. You've had your last penny out of me.

But he didn't dash out of the house to get away from me, like I had to do from my old man when I was a kid. Oh bleeding no. He let fly such a mouth of swearing from by the door that I was *shocked* at it. You could have knocked me down with a feather. I was staggered, I was. *Then* he went out. If he hadn't, I'd have half killed him.

That's what they teach 'em at school these days. Draw funny pictures. Chuck books at each other. That's what they let 'em get away with. Break arms in the playground. Kick people in. But I got him when he came back. They're not going to turn me into a walking vegetable. Waited till he closed the door behind him. Then I clocked him one. Keep your hands to yourself, he bawled, a red mark on his face.

Nearly stunned him, I had. Shook him. Served him right.

Then he laughed. He did. Rubbed his face – but he laughed at me, the bone-idle layabout. I'd have gone for him again, but he shoved his hands in his pockets and threw things at me. Right across the table. Some of 'em hit me. Others fell on the floor. A watch, and bits of money, a ring, an electric calculator, a pocket radio, two packets o' fags. My heart nearly stopped. You thieving bastard. I'll get the police, I thought. I'll get rid of him for three years. We'll all get done. But the watch I picked up was going a treat.

You told me to get something, he yelled. I hadn't said a bloody word. I never showed him how to lie. Where did he get it from? Not me. You never know where kids get to. Swap tricks at school, I suppose. Or it comes out of his mother's side of the family. We've got nowt here since you got the push, he said. What did you get it for then, eh? We all know what you got the push for – ah-ah-ah!

I get the same though from his mother. I do. Exactly the bloody same. Married her? Well, yes I did, didn't I? What are you telling me that for? I met her in a pub when I was a teddy-boy, cutting a dash in my drainpipes and sideburns. We were all teddy-boys in them days, weren't we, mate? Came back to my house to hear my Bobby Darin discs. Never looked back after that first night on the sofa. Neither of us. Bloody pity we didn't look forward. Not much o' the good stuff left. And what sort o' kids have we got?

So now I'm at home all day. Got to be, ain't I? Most of it, anyway. So we get at each other's throats. The T.V. set fizzled out. The picture spun itself to death one night, and it's still broke down. After that she didn't know what to do with herself. Neither did I, but I didn't let it bother me. I'd go out to the bookies' and see if I couldn't win a bob or two on the horses.

Never any luck, though. Win one race, lose the next. I should know better. But what else is a chap to do when he's temporarily out of work and wants to pass the time on a bit? Same when I go for a drink. Moan, moan, bleeding moan. The odd pint never broke us.

You'd better give me the money, she said, so's I can get more food on the table. Or shoes for the kids. They get plenty to eat, I said. They get free milk and buckshee dinners at school, and even extra shoes to put on their feet. They don't let 'em go hungry and barefoot these days, you know. They did once, but that was before our time. It's more than they dare do, to let it happen now.

I don't want a bloody history lesson, she said, I just want a bigger share of that money they give you at the dole office. I nearly went bloody mad at this. She wants to rob me of my last penny. Drop dead, I said. Leave me alone, or I'll knock your teeth down your chops. If you want money get some of your own. Only just don't try to cadge all of mine. I need it.

She starts screaming at this. I knew she would, but what could I do? Where do you expect me to get money? She yelled for all she was worth, so's the whole estate could hear it. There's no place I can get a penny, and you know it. I'm at my wits' end trying to think how we can get a bit extra for Christmas that'll be soon on us. The kids keep telling me what they want, and how can I get any money? They'll be going out and nicking it next.

Well, I tell her how, and she thinks I've gone mad, so I tell her again, and she thinks I'm joking, so I tell her again, and she thinks I'm rotten to the core, and I keep on telling her, but soon she runs out of the house with her hands in her ears.

I don't know! I don't know. I sometimes think I'm going to get fed up with it all. She ain't been back since. Not a word. What can you do? Can't take a joke, that's what's wrong with people. Put your foot

143

in it, whatever you might say. There's nothing left in life. No religion, no respect from your kids. Might just as well keep your trap shut. All my fault, though, that's what I know. Bound to be, ain't it?

The Devil's
Almanack

Mr G. M. Stevens, postmaster of Biddenhurst, in the
County of Kent, on Tuesday April 17th, 1866, at
exactly nine o'clock a.m., was taking readings of the
barometer, thermometer and hygrometer, and pencilling them into the blank pages of his specially
printed almanack.

As he stooped to look at the rain-gauge he noticed,
for the benefit of bird observers, that a muscular and
energetic magpie flitted from the lawn and went into
a willow tree which was just beginning to put on
leaves. Tomorrow the solemn ash would come, and
then the lime, followed by the maple, showing how
true it was that the years went on and on, yet stayed
the same.

He put a handkerchief to his nose to stem the
flood – white spots on red one day, red on white
another. He'd caught a cold (or the cold had caught
him) when he'd got into a sweat digging his garden –
or taking his readings twice a day: at nine in the
morning and nine at night, winter or summer, spring
or autumn, blue sky or blizzard, since the death of

his wife ten years ago. The heavy soil-digging had put him into a sweat, and tired him. 'Come in, Gerald,' his wife would have called when the shower commenced, if she'd been alive. And he had wanted to go in, of course, to find the time by the chronometer, and record the shower in his almanack, but the last dozen links of soil had to be turned, otherwise when would the time come again?

You recorded the weather when nothing either good or bad occurred. You filled in columns of figures every day, read dials, fitted a neat extra leg to the month's gentle or jagged graph – when you didn't want anything to happen. But for how long had this labour-hobby held life back? A drop of sweat fell into the rain-gauge, and another hit the soil.

He was short and fat, and bald at fifty, but he stood up straight, and pencilled rough calculations into his notebook. Cloud: cumulus. Amount: 7. From sun to cloud took little time when spring was a long while coming. Wind: west. You never trusted sunshine in the morning. It was beautiful, but menacing. You drank it in from the back step, the soft warm air vibrating with birds who suddenly knew why they were alive, hoping it would last but knowing it would not – the reality of birds who fed on ivy for their joy, the laudanum of sunlight for him, the sense of eternal wellbeing between waking up to take it, and going into the horrors, that fatal hiatus of any drug or drink or taste of pink-blue sky. Barometer: 29.937. Thermometer: 50. Hygrometer (Dry Bulb): 57½. (Wet Bulb): 48. Altitude: they say 400 feet, but no map shows it.

He smiled, glad the sun had gone so that he need no longer wish it would stay. Anxiety was both the spice and bane of his life. Lady Delmonden's black cat shimmered its midnight fur through the tall lawn-grass so that just its back was visible. He clapped hands but it didn't run, turned its head towards him, though he could see only its ears, and not the green-yellow eyes that managed to look so helpless and threatening at the same time. The ripple went to the hedge. Even cats are safe in Biddenhurst. It would soon be chill again.

He took the last reading and went indoors, glancing in at the parlour where his daughter Emily's body was neatly tucked on to the beige chaise-longue.

There had been no need for it, but there never is. He went into his study. God fulfils our needs, as we fulfil God's, and providing the compact is kept by all His creatures great and small – as well as by Him – we have no cause for fear in this life. But it troubled Stevens for a moment that he was worried by it – after promising himself that he wouldn't be. May the Good Lord strike me dead, he sighed.

He smiled at such a predicament, but became easy as he put in his last observation of the morning. Closing the specially bound fully-ruled logbook from the stationer's in Tunbridge Wells was a beautiful manoeuvre of finality, prelude to opening it again. In one compartment of his desk were half a dozen letters from Lady Delmonden to her son who started two weeks ago with his regiment for Gibraltar. Because he kept them neatly, their presence did not intimidate him. Their journey ended here, of necessity a short one, instead of where they were sent – those slim packets of tearful pleadings which he'd never thought would come from that tall, frigid, ugly woman.

Her soldier son was lean and fair, and ugly too. Disagreeable, until he chose to smile which – by its very rarity, like a primrose in bleak November – charmed the unwary or the stranger.

Emily had heard him kicking snow from his boots at the scraper outside, before he walked in with letters for the evening post. Counting stamps, she forgot whereabouts her finger had been on them when he demanded some for himself. That must have been how it started. From his study just behind, he'd heard the loud and throaty voice, but went on working out his average temperatures and comparing this year's monthly pressures with last year's. Had he been there to serve him would God have made it any different? If not that day, then another. Each day was the same, except for his recordings of the weather.

A sharp angle of shadow sliced the garden into light on one side and dimness on the other. White spots of daisies on either part, some blessed and the same amount not, and no one to say the why or wherefore of it. Perhaps the wind would change, bring back the sun to stay, feed the leaves and dry the grass, ruffle the cat's fur that once more walked across the lawn towards the kitchen garden, stalking all movement.

He came often after that, laughing as he bought more stamps, improperly confiding that he'd fallen in love and needed to send her letters every day, which put Emily off her guard while opening her eyes to him.

The heart would ache but never burst. The blood rose like burning paraffin. John would get no letters from his mother whilever he was postmaster here, unless by a fluke she dropped them in another town – though she was the sort of woman who these days would grieve only at home. Neither would she get any Royal Mail from him if he could stop it. In any case Delmonden, for all his show to Emily, was no writer of letters, cared only for his pleasures at other people's heartbreaks.

His one letter back which he had intercepted, and held open now to read again, was posted to his mother, and said that he, John Delmonden, after waiting a long time for a suitable ship at Weymouth, and then the appropriate weather, found that the army's dispositions had been changed, and that his regiment was ordered back to Dover – not far from Biddenhurst – so he would gallop over the Romney Marsh and come up through Appledore and Wittersham to see Emily Stevens.

'And mother, no matter what you say about her being below my station, I mean to marry her, and nothing will stop me, so set *your* mind to it as well. As you, and I suppose everybody by this time knows, we were married enough already – and now I aim to make it final. God willed I should not leave for Gibraltar, and I know His voice – by God! – when I hear it. Anyway, I shall go to her first when I get to Biddenhurst.'

No, he was such an engine as did not know what it was doing. At the same time he was as feeling as the barometer and the thermometer, the hygrometer and clock and calendar put together, only he was not responsible for moving the measurements of them. Everybody had their feelings, but thought little of their effect on others unless they knew God was reading and recording them hour by hour – and there were devils who did not care, even then.

How long could it go on? The columns of his readings made no sense. He closed the book, and gripped Lady Delmonden's letters to her son in his left hand, wanting to eat them, burn them, throw the bundle out through the rain at the stalking black cat with pink ribbon round its neck.

Ever since Emily was born he had been afraid of losing her, of her catching fever or consumption. After her mother died, his black dreams turned on the taps of his own sweat at night. With blankets up and blinds drawn they harassed him in the darkest sleep, till he awoke happy it was all unreal – but weak, though able to go to her room where she slept, and look in at her untroubled face.

The earth wasn't generous in giving breath, because it wanted all people walking about to be under its soil and feeding it. It was the greed of the earth that made it beautiful. Life was a thin join of air in every body. What the Lord provides He takes away, but was it the earth, or was it God?

The soil gives abundantly to ivy tendrils and leaves, a parasitic growth whose coils lap as thick as pythons around tree-trunks and suck the tree's sap, till it dies and falls into a heap of dust to feed the earth. Likewise, ivy destroys a house. That picturesque green mat at the wall is a many-armed monster sent up by the rich vindictive earth to bring all things level with it.

Five drops of laudanum would not be enough – nor even fifty. He took the first letter of the bundle and tore it into confetti, and let it fall over the face of Emily. Her lips were thinner, the nose small and narrower at the bone than it had been, the forehead like paper. Be careful what you dread, in case you bring it to pass. But what you dread is only a warning of what the future has in store. Does God look over us from that far back?

Her face and form were littered with the paper bits of John Delmonden's letter. When he'd pushed the pillow against her mouth it was only to stop his own agony at what she had told him. He began pressing in order to hide her face, and went on with all his force when she was beyond consciousness because he couldn't bear the thought of her coming back and reproaching him for what he was doing.

Rain was tapping on the window. Perhaps the Romney Marsh would swallow Delmonden up for what he'd done. His hands were pale and puffy, and trembled as he tore the month of April out of his almanack, and made the scraps of that descend to join the other. The air was sweetening, the glass falling, the pressure a great weight on his eyes.

Each separate bone was bitterly tired. He steadied himself by the wall, the paper now the colour of laudanum, belladonna, gin, recalling how four years ago Lady Delmonden had quipped that such a widower as he get married again, that it was sinful to stay single on God's earth. Wasn't he lonely?

'I have my daughter to keep me company,' he answered – but she looked very strange at that.

A maid of hers would need a husband soon, she said, young, able, and bonny too. Perhaps he should have flowed with it – he tore March out as well, and the stitching came loose – but some stubborn notion gripped him, and he said no, and she was thwarted in her idea, so walked out cold-faced but polite, and never mentioned it again. But there'd been hidden pleading in her icy eyes. Six months later that same maid had a bastard drawn out of her, and who the lover was no one knew, except for certain hints about her roaming son.

Such a festering entered his vision when Emily told him the real truth of the tale he'd dreaded hearing when she came back five days after going with John Delmonden, and he joined it to the pictures in his own mind, and to Lady Delmonden's rigid face, and to her son's smile, and then to his new-found rage, and picked up the cushion because he couldn't bear the sight of tears on her cheeks. Was it only to wipe them gently away?

February and January, back to the hinges of the year. On January 1st there had been no cloud in the sky, a brilliant and empty blue all day, after the full moon of the night. What was the weather any more to him? Every subtle change of heat and sky he'd analysed, but what of the world inside his own flesh and blood, and that continent behind the pale blue eyes of Emily? It was all mystery, and his life had been an unchanging day that defied reading because

he was locked blindly in his own brand of unknow-
ing. The more you hide your soul from others the
more it becomes hidden from yourself. But why
hadn't he seen that until now?

He'd known she was dead, for ever and irrevo-
cably, the moment he lifted the cushion, and so the
calm of understanding took him under its protection.
But as the hours went by he became less certain that
she'd never talk to him again, and while taking his
meteorological readings in the garden he forgot completely that she would not be walking about the
house when he went back to it.

Bending down, he put his ear to her breast to see if
any pulse was there. The feeling that someone would
never come back again – all that his life meant to
him – was replaced by the certainty that there were,
after all, momentous things still to come.

One by one he pulled his almanacks to pieces and
piled them into the parlour fireplace. He felt the
excitement of a criminal as he knelt on the rug and
shaped them down with his hand before lighting.
Perhaps the flames would tell him something, the
heat speak to the heat within. Emily moved – but it
was a ball of paper to one side of the main heap,
twisted by an unseen flame that had crept on an
undercurrent towards it.

The enclosed space, the warm room he'd been
used to with his wife and through his marriage, the
semaphoring flame on the opposite wall, and Emily
lying quietly on the chaise-longue, filled him with a
joy of life such as he'd never felt. The music swirling
and roaring fed his fibres, and blotted out memory so
that his feelings were caged into this room and
moment.

If there had been real music the ground would
have opened more and he would have danced into it,
a waltz for his feet, a gavotte for his arms, a minuet
for his lips and eyes. But to feel the new rush of hope

he sat on a straight walnut-backed chair midway between Emily and the fire, a final quietness in which he sampled the meaning of his past life. It held the agonies at bay, wolves beyond the windows and the wind.

The final black paper-ash crumbled. A draught came down the chimney and swirled it. When the birds stopped he heard its noise. It was a fair, fine day. The nothing-rain had passed over, only a threat. The curtains didn't meet, and a long sliver of sunlight hung from the ceiling.

A neighing horse outside displaced other noises, and he sat still, earmarked by the gap between its stopping and footsteps which ended with a knock against the side door. He reached to the shelf for his loaded pistol, and put it into his jacket pocket. Never let anyone know that you suspect them. Always keep secret those innermost perturbations that might otherwise ruffle the waters of their treacherous calm. Leave them in peace till the time comes to strike. The barometer's needle was set for a few days of good weather.

The knocking sounded again, and he sat down. It could be three times for all he cared – and would be. Let him hammer with his pampered fist. He didn't beat so loud when he came for Emily. He was an ill the world could well be purged of. Tears burst from his eyes when he looked at her. He'd heard them say that he was a wild man, but that meant he'd been afraid too long, set off for church too often perhaps, walking there with his back straight, but returning on his hands and feet. You can never get your revenge on someone who has given the first blow. Forget it, by destroying them.

He smiled, and stood as the third rapping began, walked through his study to the door and pulled it open. The hinges squeaked, alive. Everything had its own noise.

'What's wrong with you, Stevens? You must open the place. Are you ill?' Lady Delmonden pushed her way in. 'I *won't* stand outside.'

He felt the comforting hard weight of the pistol against his bone, his mind splintered at the shock of seeing her. She held an umbrella, as if to lean on it. 'Tell me' – she was taller, her finger lifted – 'has Emily had any word from my son?'

He knew he would have to speak, move his tongue with the same force as his arm when hard at digging. 'She tells me nothing.'

'I don't suppose she does, but I'll speak to her myself.'

'No' – he hadn't intended to say anything.

'Won't I? You must curb your temper, Stevens.'

If he didn't speak, he would shoot. 'No, I tell you.'

'Do you know what you're saying?'

He searched out his words, because he had never lied: 'She went on the coach to Tunbridge Wells. I'll send her to you as soon as she comes back.'

'Are you all right?' Her horse neighed again outside, a footman holding the reins.

'Yes.'

'Make sure you do, then. I can't be kept in the dark like this by the pair of them. Good day to you.' A final turn of rage brought her back: 'And next time I call on you, you will ask me into your parlour. Do you understand?'

'Yes, my lady.'

What did those blue eyes with the pale dead skin around them know? He looked as long as he dared into the waterfall of sky, as if he would collapse, hoping she would go, for his hand was on the cool handle of the gun. When she had come to him, and touted her pregnant maid, he had created in himself a complete scheme saying that really she wanted him to marry her, and this was her devious way of testing the ground for it. In her young years there had been stories of her runawayings and heart-stormings, but he knew that they were as nothing compared to his if he brewed up such ridiculous ideas as this. Who am I? he asked now, as he had then. I saw her first when she came with her mother, carrying a basket of cakes to the village school.

'Send her to me, then,' she told him.

He closed the door, and went back to his parlour.

Primroses, sorrel, violets and celandines were in Oldpark Wood, but he'd no energy to go and search out a few. As a child Emily had laid a bunch on his desk one spring. It's an inhuman machine that won't let you bring back such tender moments in all their reality. He smelled the soil as he pulled them up by the roots. He pondered on it in his fixity when even his eyeballs wouldn't move though he wanted them to. Hands on thighs, legs slightly apart, a scene set for his immobile head, waiting for Emily to breathe again.

Hours drew out. There was no time to act because time did not exist. On the sea the waves were molten metal, thin, without smoke. The motion and the endlessness made him sick.

Someone had come into the house. His eyes moved, sending a fissure of life back to his fingers. It was all plain now, and he called Emily in a normal voice, as if she would run to him. A chair went over in the study. He wished he had strewn her with flowers instead of those plague spots of paper bits.

'Emily!' Delmonden called.

He stood, and waited, awake again, calm even, but with a faint sweaty smile as if he'd turned back into a child. He wanted to be friendly and answer him, but was sly enough in his stunned and stunted childishness to know that if he did the frame of his new-found tenuous manhood would fall apart. For the first time he was aware of the clock ticking on the wall, and thought it must have stopped yesterday, and for some unaccountable reason started again this second, it was so loud and disturbing as it hammered inside him.

The door was gently opened, and the floor creaked as Delmonden looked in. He tried not to stare at him, and turned aside.

'Why the devil didn't you tell me you were here? I don't want to see over your whole damned house.'

He was of the tall people who could walk in, and look for his daughter, sidestepping any man's freedom and dignity. There was no life without Emily. He wasn't afraid of him – as he had been when he watched the whole plot forming but told himself that his brain spun false pictures. What else is there to live for if you've stopped being afraid?

'What do you want?' – surprised at the clearness of his voice. He stood between the door and the chaise-longue.

Delmonden must have ridden hard. His cloak was open – a dark suit under it, pale waistcoat, white shirt up to his throat, a florid ill-formed face just out of youth, a long clean-shaven chin. 'Why don't you let daylight in the place? Where is she?'

He stepped backwards to the shelf, a hand at ease in his pocket. 'She's not well.'

Delmonden came forward. He saw the road in front of him, pot-holes whose water reflected the variable sky. The rhythm of hooves still rang in his hearing. His eyes almost touched her forehead. 'I'll get the doctor. For God's sake, why didn't *you*?'

'She's dead.'

He felt his finger on the curve. It was like a hook, and the handle tilted, hidden. Forgive me, Lord: I know exactly what I do. The clock behind him seemed to explode, a noise blowing paper into the air as the bullet flew, a great stone at Delmonden's stomach.

He screamed, hands to the pain. He wanted to ask a question, but changed his mind: 'You devil! She hated you. I can see . . . '

The second ball hit him, this time the whole white of the sun before he fell.

Mr G. M. Stevens, late postmaster of Biddenhurst, was hanged at eight o'clock a.m. on June 6th at Maidstone Gaol, in the County of Kent.

When about to be executed the crowd threw soil and dung at him. He saw these gestures merely as the earth extending a hand, welcoming him to become part of the good fellowship of the loam. The people were enraged by his indifference, because the trial revealed the abominations he had practised on the bodies of his victims. He had been able to keep them a further day before Lady Delmonden's tenants broke in and found them.

As the mob pelted him, he remained silent, looking at the sky, and feeling the air on his face. It was a south-west wind. The cloud: nimbus. Amount: 10. Temperature (as far as he could tell): 50. The parson had been good enough to inform him, before beginning his futile prayers, that the barometer read 29.620. A slight rain was falling.

His left hand reached for his almanack, and the crowd roared when it swung into the air.

The Fiddle

On the banks of the sinewy River Leen, where it flowed through Radford, stood a group of cottages called Harrison's Row. There must have been six to eight of them, all in a ruinous condition, but lived in nevertheless.

They had been put up for stockingers during the Industrial Revolution a hundred years before, so that by now the usual small red English housebricks had become weatherstained and, in some places, almost black.

Harrison's Row had a character all of its own, both because of its situation, and the people who lived there. Each house had a space of pebbly soil rising in front, and a strip of richer garden sloping away from the kitchen door down to the diminutive River Leen at the back. The front gardens had almost merged into one piece of common ground, while those behind had in most cases retained their separate plots.

As for the name of the isolated row of cottages, nobody knew who Harrison had been, and no one was ever curious about it. Neither did they know where the Leen came from, though some had a general idea as to where it finished up.

A rent man walked down cobblestoned Leen Place every week to collect what money he could. This wasn't much, even at the best of times which, in the 'thirties', were not too good – though no one in their conversation was able to hark back to times when they had been any better.

From the slight rise on which the houses stood, the back doors and windows looked across the stream into green fields, out towards the towers and pinnacles of Wollaton Hall in one direction, and the woods of Aspley Manor in the other.

After a warm summer without much rain the children were able to wade to the fields on the other side. Sometimes they could almost paddle. But after a three-day downpour when the air was still heavy with undropped water, and coloured a menacing gun-metal blue, it was best not to go anywhere near the river, for one false slip and you would get sucked in, and be dragged by the powerful current along to the Trent some miles away. In that case there was no telling where you'd end up. The water seemed to flow into the River Amazon itself, indicated by the fact that Frankie Buller swore blind how one day he had seen a crocodile snapping left and right downstream with a newborn baby in its mouth. You had to be careful – and that was a fact. During the persistent rain of one autumn water came up over the gardens and almost in at the back doors.

Harrison's Row was a cut-off place in that not many people knew about it unless they were familiar with the district. You went to it along St Peter's Street, and down Leen Place. But it was delightful for the kids who lived there because out of the back gardens they could go straight into the stream of the Leen. In summer an old tin hip bath would come from one of the houses. Using it for a boat, and stripped to their white skins, the children were happy while sun and weather lasted.

The youths and older kids would eschew this fun and set out in a gang, going far beyond, to a bend of the canal near Wollaton Pit where the water was warm – almost hot – due to some outlet from the mine itself. This place was known as ''otties', and they'd stay all day with a bottle of lemonade and a piece of bread, coming back late in the evening looking pink and tired as if out of a prolonged dipping in the ritual bath. But a swim in 'otties was only for the older ones, because a boy of four had once been drowned there.

Harrison's Row was the last of Nottingham where it met the countryside. Its houses were at the very edge of the city, in the days before those numerous housing estates had been built beyond. The line of dwellings called Harrison's Row made a sort of outpost bastion before the country began.

Yet the houses in the city didn't immediately start behind, due to gardens and a piece of wasteground, which gave to Harrison's Row a feeling of isolation. It stood somewhat on its own, as if the city intended one day to leapfrog over it and obliterate the country beyond.

On the other hand, any foreign army attacking from the west, over the green fields that glistened in front, would first have to flatten Harrison's Row before getting into the innumerable streets of houses behind.

Across the Leen, horses were sometimes to be seen in the fields and, in other fields beyond, the noise of combine harvesters could be heard at work in the summer. Children living there, and adults as well, had the advantage of both town and country. On a fine evening late in August one of the unemployed husbands might be seen looking across at the noise of some machinery working in a field, his cap on but wearing no shirt, as if wondering why he was here and not over there, and why in fact he had ever left those same fields in times gone by to be forced into this bit of a suburb where he now had neither work nor purpose in life. He was not bitter, and not much puzzled perhaps, yet he couldn't help being envious of those still out there in the sunshine.

In my visions of leaving Nottingham for good – and they were frequent in those days – I never reckoned on doing so by the high road or railway. Instead I saw myself wading or swimming the Leen from Harrison's Row, and setting off west once I was on the other side.

A tale remembered with a laugh at that time told about how young Ted Griffin, who had just started work, saw two policemen one day walking down Leen Place towards Harrison's Row. Convinced they had to come to arrest him for meter-breaking, he ran through the house and garden, went over the fence, jumped into the Leen – happily not much swollen – waded across to the field, then four-legged it over the railway, and made his way to Robins Wood a mile or so beyond. A perfect escape route. He stayed two days in hiding, and then crept home at night, famished and soaked, only to find that the police had not come for him, but to question Blonk next door, who was suspected of poaching. When they did get Ted Griffin he was pulled out of bed one morning even before he'd had time to open his eyes and think about a spectacular escape across the Leen.

Jeff Bignal was a young unmarried man of twenty-four. His father had been killed in the Great War, and he lived with his mother at Number Six Harrison's Row, and worked down nearby Radford Pit. He was short in height, and plump, his white skin scarred back and front with livid blue patches where he had been knocked with coal at the mine face.

161

When he went out on Saturday night he brilliantined his hair.

After tea in summer while it was still light and warm he would sit in his back garden playing the fiddle, and when he did everybody else came out to listen. Or they opened the doors and windows so that the sound of his music drifted in, while the woman stayed at the sink or wash-copper, or the man at his odd jobs. Anyone with a wireless would turn it down or off.

Even tall dark sallow-faced elderly Mrs Deaffy (a kid sneaked into her kitchen one day and thieved her last penny-packet of cocoa and she went crying to tell Mrs Atkin who, when her youngest came in, hit him so hard with her elbow that one of his teeth shot out and the blood washed away most of the cocoa-stains around his mouth) – old Mrs Deaffy stood by her back door as if she weren't stone deaf any more and could follow each note of Jeffrey Bignal's exquisite violin. She smiled at seeing everyone occupied, fixed or entranced, and therefore no torment to herself, which was music enough to her whether she could hear it or not.

And Blonk, in the secretive dimness of the kitchen, went on mending his poaching nets before setting out with Arthur Bede next door on that night's expedition to Gunthorpe by the banks of the Trent, where the green escarpment between there and Kneeton was riddled with warrens and where, so it was said, if you stood sufficiently still the rabbits ran over your feet, and it was only necessary to make a quick grab to get one.

Jeff sat on a chair, oblivious to everybody, fed up with his day's work at the pit and only wanting to lose himself in his own music. The kids stopped splashing and shouting in the water, because if they didn't they might get hauled in and clouted with just the right amount of viciousness to suit the crime and the occasion. It had happened before, though Jeff had always been too far off to notice.

His face was long, yet generally cheerful – contrary to what one would expect – a smile settling on it whenever he met and passed anybody on the street, or on his way to the group of shared lavatories at the end of the Row. But his face was almost down and lost to the world as he sat on his chair and brought forth his first sweet notes of a summer's evening.

It was said that a neighbour in the last place they had lived had taught him to play like that. Others maintained it was an uncle who had shown him how. But nobody knew for sure because when some-one asked directly he said that if he had any gift at all it must have come from God above. It was known that on some Sundays of the year, if the sun was out, he went to the Methodist chapel on St Peter's Street.

He could play anything from 'Greensleeves' to 'Mademoiselle from Armentières'. He could do a beautiful heart-pulling version of Handel's *Largo*, and throw in bits from *The Messiah* as well. He would go from one piece to another with no rhyme or reason, from ridiculousness to sublimity, with almost shocking abruptness, but as the hour or so went by it all appeared easy and natural, part of a long piece coming from Jeff Bignal's fiddle while the ball of the sun went down behind his back.

To a child it seemed as if the songs lived in the hard collier's muscle at the top of his energetic arm, and that they queued one by one to get out. Once free, they rushed along his flesh from which the shirtsleeves had been rolled up, and split into his fingertips, where they were played out with ease into the warm evening air.

The grass in the fields across the stream was livid and lush, almost blue, and a piebald horse stood with bent head, eating oats out of a large old pram whose wheels had long since gone. The breeze wafted across from places farther out, from Robins Wood and the Cherry Orchard, Wollaton Roughs and Bramcote Hills and even, on a day that was not too hot, from the tops of the Pennines in Derbyshire.

Jeff played for himself, for the breeze against his arm, for the soft hiss of the flowing Leen at the end of the garden, and maybe also for the horse in the field, which took no notice of anything and which, having grown tired of its oats in the pram, bent its head over the actual grass and began to roam in search of succulent pastures.

In the middle of the winter Jeff's fiddling was forgotten. He went into the coal mine before it was light, and came up only after it had got dark. Walking down Leen Place, he complained to Blonk that it was hard on a man not to see daylight for weeks at a time.

'That's why I wain't go anywhere near the bleddy pit,' Blonk said vehemently, though he had worked there from time to time, and would do so again when harried by his wife and children. 'You'd do better to come out on a bit o' poaching with me and Arthur,' he suggested.

It was virtually true that Jeff saw no daylight, because even on Sunday he stayed in bed most of the day, and if it happened to be dull there was little enough sky to be seen through his front bedroom window, which looked away from the Leen and up the hill.

The upshot of his complaint was that he would do anything to change such a situation. A man was less than an animal for putting up with it.

'I'd do anything,' he repeated to his mother over his tea in the single room downstairs.

'But what, though?' she asked. 'What can you do, Jeff?'

'Well, how do I know?' he almost snapped at her. 'But I'll do summat, you can be sure of that.'

He didn't do anything till the weather got better and life turned a bit sweeter. Maybe this improvement finally got him going, because it's hard to help yourself towards better things when you're too far down in the dumps.

On a fine blowy day with both sun and cloud in the sky Jeff went out in the morning, walking up Leen Place with his fiddle under his arm. The case had been wiped and polished.

In the afternoon he came back without it.

'Where's your fiddle?' Ma Jones asked.

He put an awkward smile on to his pale face, and told her: 'I sold it.'

'Well I never! How much for?'

He was too shocked at her brazen question not to tell the truth: 'Four quid.'

'That ain't much.'

'It'll be enough,' he said roughly.

'Enough for what, Jeff?'

He didn't say, but the fact that he had sold his fiddle for four quid rattled up and down the line of cottages till everybody knew of it. Others swore he'd got ten pounds for it, because something that made such music must be worth more than a paltry four, and in any case Jeff would never say how much he'd really got for it, for fear that someone would go in and rob him.

They wondered why he'd done it, but had to wait for the answer, as one usually does. But there was nothing secretive about Jeff Bignal, and if he'd sold his music for a mess of pottage he saw no point in not letting them know why. They'd find out sooner or later, anyway.

All he'd had to do was make up his mind, and he'd done that lying on his side at the pit face while ripping coal out with his pick and shovel. Decisions

165

made like that can't be undone, he knew. He'd
brooded on it all winter, till the fact of having settled
it seemed to have altered the permanent expression
of his face, and given it a new look which caused
people to wonder whether he would ever be able to
play the fiddle again anyway – at least with his old
spirit and dash.

With the four quid he paid the first week's rent on
a butcher's shop on Denman Street, and bought a
knife, a chopper, and a bit of sharpening stone, as
well as a wooden block. Maybe he had a quid or two
more knocking around, though if he had it couldn't
have been much, but with four quid and a slice of
bluff he got enough credit from a wholesaler at the
meat market downtown to stock his shop with
mutton and beef, and in a couple of days he was in
trade. The people of Harrison's Row were amazed at
how easy it was, though nobody had ever thought of
doing it themselves.

Like a serious young man of business Mr Bignal –
as he was now known – parted his hair down the
middle, so that he didn't look so young any more,
but everyone agreed that it was better than being at
Radford Pit. They'd seen how he had got fed-up with
selling the sweat of his brow.

No one could say that he prospered, but they
couldn't deny that he made a living. And he didn't
have to suffer the fact of not seeing daylight for
almost the whole of the winter.

Six months after opening the shop he got married.
The reception was held at the chapel on St Peter's
Street, which seemed to be a sort of halfway house
between Harrison's Row on the banks of the Leen
and the butcher's shop on Denman Street farther
up.

Everybody from Harrison's Row was invited for a
drink and something to eat; but he knew them too
well to let any have either chops or chitterlings (or

even black puddings) on tick when they came into his shop.

The people of Harrison's Row missed the sound of his fiddle on long summer evenings, though the children could splash and shout with their tin bath-tub undisturbed, floundering through shallows and scrambling up to grass on the other bank, and wondering what place they'd reach if they walked without stopping till it got dark.

Two years later the Second World War began, and not long afterwards meat as well as nearly everything else was put on the ration. Apart from which, Jeff was only twenty-six, so got called up into the army. He never had much chance to make a proper start in life, though people said that he came out all right in the end.

The houses of Harrison's Row were condemned as unfit to live in, and a bus depot stands on the site.

The packed mass of houses on the hill behind – forty years after Jeff Bignal sold his violin – is also vanishing, and high rise hencoops (as the people call them) are put in their place. The demolition crew knock down ten houses a day – though the foreman told me there was still work for another two years.

Some of the houses would easily have lasted a few more decades, for the bricks were perfect, but as the foreman went on: 'You can't let them stand in the way of progress' – whatever that means.

The people have known each other for generations but, when they are moved to their new estates and blocks of flats, they will know each other for genera-tions more, because as I listen to them talking, they speak a language which, in spite of everything and everyone, never alters.

The Gate of a Great Mansion

Fruit boxes were pounded against the shore by a snaking band of oil-logged water. The wood of the boxes was grey, hitting the rocks till it was splintered and stringy. Dead logs were covered in tar. Rotting offal, swirling from the town and jetties, was re-shaped and hardened into a kind of pumice by the battering ebb and flow of the wash. A stench hit the nostrils like ice when the wind veered full in the face. He lit a second pipe before the bowl was cold.

The whole flank of a three-funnelled steamer had gone to rust. Coolies going to work in the tin mines and rubber plantations of Malaya were so crowded on deck that it was hard to see where the mass of people ended and the superstructure began. One day the hulk will vanish in a typhoon, he thought, and the owners will retire on the insurance. A drum of paint costs treble what it does in Europe. Everyone says that business is bad, and they are right. You go inland for hemp, tea and timber, and get little or nothing when you bring them out. When it gets dark a clean wind pushes the stench aside.

The last chord of the sun's red disc was sucked behind the mountains. Take me with you, he said, when it wasn't so far down that it might not hear. He wanted sharp hooks that he could throw out to it for a free ride. He looked at the indigo sea chopping beyond his feet, and into the inky maw of the wider bottle. Nothing is free. Beyond the throat of rocks were stars. A lantern glowed at the prow of a sampan that went slowly towards the steamer. The peasants were dying from Revolution, Consumption and Cholera. They sleep-walk after imbibing the vile poppy dust of opium. Wireless telegraphy from Europe talks of war and prices.

He wanted only rain whenever he felt fever or influenza pushing his senses to their limits. The sun was on its way out, but one day it would come back to burn the world. The rain's cooling wash would flow down the veranda and along the gutters, would run through his veins and clear sludge from the mind, extinguish the unwholesome nightmare all around. He could only think when he was ill, yet his mind turned against him at such times. It must have been during similar feverish bouts that he had gone through the motions of coming to Amoy. He would not forget the smell of drying fish, even a hundred years after he had died.

Today he had been paid, and bought a sports jacket, so that there weren't enough dollars left for the instalment on his room. Both space and jackets were dear – for Europeans. Perhaps I can hold the landlord back till next month. Disturb him from his game of sticks and coins and a row of little books. Play it as long as you like, but I won't be here. If he throws me out, he'll get nothing, because you can't get taels (nor even *cash*) from a beggar. He's heard it often in the last year, but his look will say nothing yet all the same will say: a merchant's clerk isn't worth much. A Chinese can do the work better, and for less. Except that Poynter-Davis wouldn't trust one, though God knows why.

He walked. He was getting nowhere. The first sign of a fever was that the pipe tasted as if it were filled with a well-mixed compound of shit and soot. He was glad when it burned away and he could knock out the dottle. His mother didn't know what her brother did for a living out here, only that he was 'doing well' – that magic phrase which was supposed to open every gate for the rest of the family. Nobody was 'doing well'. The Japanese were machine-gunning and bombing their sure way through Manchuria. The world was worn out. He stepped carefully in the dark. The noise of rats squeaking and scuffling away from his shoes made him feel that he was not entirely set apart from the world. He could no longer see the rusting flank of the decrepit steamer that would sink in a monsoon if it took him to England. It would be no easier trying for a job in Singapore or Penang.

He coughed from day to day, but illness was a fraud. Even if you were half dead you couldn't allow yourself to feel so at thirty-five. There were plenty of lights in the town. There was life. Amoy wasn't un-healthy any more. The old hands laughed, and spoke about heaps of corpses. The old always swore that things were better for everybody than they had been in their youth, but it only meant they had grown more tolerant of misery – or become richer on it.

Even the Chinese smiled. He hated himself when he shouted. Things were said to be difficult in England. There was no work. There was the dole for everybody. They used the word to terrify. If you came home, you'd go on the dole, they wrote. In any case, he didn't totally dislike it *here*. The stench of the town on one side and the odorous piss of sea on the other were homely enough, but his thoughts were caught in the unceasing and remorseless bang of the surf.

Letters were nearly two months getting home. He wrote every week, still the anxious boy who bothered them with mail. If they didn't look at the date they could imagine each letter took no more than seven days. *He* would have done, in their places. They'd be happier hearing only four times a year. His father at the bank and his mother at home were, in their old fashioned way, waiting for him to make a fortune in Amoy. Or Shanghai. Or Tientsin. Or Foochow. Anywhere, as long as he was out of the way. From the squalor of human souls you were supposed to get rich.

He could go back if his father died, and live with her. He never would. She loved him too much, she said, but would bore him to death because she hated him. He couldn't even go back into himself, not as he was before he came out. He would never find his own spirit as long as he stayed in Amoy. This country was too big. He had never known himself, even in a small place. It wouldn't be possible in the sort of life his father had always led, either. Six hundred pounds a year and a Morris car, and sending in the *People* crossword every week for sixpence.

He was jostled as he made his way towards the Bund. Coolies with stinking breath pushed against him. His tongue was rancid from fever. A hand went towards his pocket but he knocked it away. His Swan fountain pen was taken just after he arrived, but now he was forever on the look-out. A pair of eyes coming towards him showed the intentions of the mind that lived behind them. They understood each other, so he was safe. He, in his weakness, could ram with his shoulder, choking on the bad language that wouldn't leave his throat. Crowds always threatened when he wanted to be alone.

Sixteen years ago, walls of wet mud seeped through revetted fresh-smelling planks in Flanders. Walking the zig-zags of his sector, he had forced his way between the members of his platoon waiting to go over the top. That place too had been crowded, but he had felt good to be there. It was small enough in which to know himself. He could tell who he was, clambering the springy ladder and into the open as if into the unlit afternoon attic of a vast house visited as children. Would a ghost leap? A scimitar swing to chop off your legs? It hadn't. It was good.

He hoped his men would follow. They did. The scimitar got most of them, but it was better there than in school. A patriotic patrol cost fifty men. Life had become dimmer since. Nobody would follow him any more, which he understood because he couldn't even follow himself, since the only self he might have followed had vanished long ago. If it hadn't he would still not have known where to go.

At the height of his fever's influence (no one had diagnosed it, but only he knew a lassitude without pain or headache that had stricken him for no reason and vibrated as far as his brain) he had dreamed he was on a small flat-bottomed boat going between the high walls of the Yangtse Gorges beyond Ichang. He'd only heard the old hands talk of them, of the fact that the river was so boxed in by gorges that the sun could not be seen except at noon, and the moon only at its highest meridian.

But in his dream he was lying happily back, no oars rowing, no motor drumming, no diesel reek or anyone punting him through or pulling perilously from the shore, but going on and on towards the west as if travelling by a benign and co-operative current. In places the river banks sloped away and he could see the huts of a porters' village, or fisher-boats drawn up on the gravel. People waved, at first friendly and then warning him with more than menace if he didn't take notice.

The broad and often devastating flow of the Yangtse was east to the China Sea and the Pacific, but here he was on a current running him *west* through the heart of China. Fever played tricks with the soles of the feet, invented geographical flukes, altered the course of rivers and spun the cardinal points of the world. Fever made humanity feel that it might one day be possible to do the same.

He passed the kitchen, a jigsaw puzzle of culinary gewgaws. He got to his room, and lay down. Hunger was an act of spite on the part of the body. It reminded you to keep on living, and laughed like a demon when you did so.

The 'old hands' in their armchairs at the club, or in the lounge of the King George Hotel, mooned on about 'the China that we used to know, and how damned sad to see it change.' The more obvious it was that their days were numbered the more they thought the misery was picturesque. In reality it consisted of endless landscapes that dying coolies carried them through in their palanquins. They talked of bringing out turmeric and sugar from beyond Chungking, of transporting amber from the north, as well as getting bristles and silk from the wilds of Szechwan.

But in the dining room they also recalled the alluvial plains of great estuaries that kill as surely as famine. The moon rises and sets on destitution. Things he heard almost brought up the vomit. Some of the merchants were virtuosos in their sexual predilections.

Amoy was the gate of a great mansion, but it was a paper house, and the inside was rotten. From his bed he saw only the fire, the burning down, flames spreading and enveloping, that did not scorch when he put out his hands. He heard the crack of burning wood from the interior, and great sparks spitting

173

fearfully out with the energy that only fire could give as huge beams collapsed, and cleaned everything, curing all hungers, even his own.

A Time to Keep

Martin drew the cloth from the kitchen table. An old tea-stain made a map of Greenland when held up to the light. He folded it into an oblong and laid it on the dresser.

After the anxiety of getting his brother and sister to bed he lifted his books from the cupboard and spread them over the bare wood, where they would stay till the heart-catching click of the gate latch signalled his parents' return.

He was staying in to see that the fire did not go out, and to keep the light on. He was staying up because he was older. When that unmistakable click of the gate latch sounded he would set a kettle on the gas to make coffee. Funny how thirsty they still were after being in the boozer all night. His two-hour dominion over the house would be finished, but as consolation he could give in to the relief of knowing that they had not after all been hit by a bus and killed.

Most of the books had been stolen. None had been read from end to end. When opened they reeked of

175

damp from bookshop shelves. Or they stank from
years of storage among plant pots and parlour soot.

He put a French grammar on to *Peveril of the Peak*,
and a Bible in Polish on top of that. The clock could
be heard now that they were out and he had ex-
tinguished the television. He sang a tune to its
ticking under his breath, then went back to his
books. He would start work next year, and didn't
know whether he wanted to or not. Things could go on
like this for ever as far as he was concerned. You got
booted out of school, though, at fifteen, and that was
that.

The certainty that one day he would be pushed
into a job had hovered around him since he first
realised as a child that his father went out every
morning in order to earn money with which to feed
them, pay the rent, get clothes, and keep a roof over
their heads. His mother used these phrases, and they
stabbed into him like fire. At that time work had
nothing to do with him, but it soon would have. It
was a place of pay and violence which his father
detested, to judge by the look on his face when he
came home every evening with his snapsack and tea-
can.

Under the dark space of the stairs he shovelled
around for coal to bank up the dull fire – a pleasurable task, as long as the flames came back to life. A
hole in the pan needed bigger lumps set over it so
that cobbles and slack wouldn't spill on the mat
between coal-heap and grate. They'd rather have a
few pints of beer than buy a dustpan.

He washed his hands in the scullery. He liked soap
that was keen to the smell. Arranging his chair, he
sat down again and lifted the cover of a beige leather-
bound volume of French magazines. He read a
sentence under the picture: a bridge over the River
Seine near Rouen. In other books he was able to put
Portuguese or Italian phrases into English. When a

word appealed to his sight he manoeuvred through the alphabet of a dictionary to get at its meaning, though he never tried to learn a language properly. He handled books like a miser. In each one his name was written in capital letters, though there was no danger of them being stolen, because they were gold that could not be spent. The strange kind of hunger he felt in looking at them often fixed him into a hypnosis that stopped him using them properly.

If burglars came they would nick the television, not books. They were stacked according to size, then sorted in their various languages. Excitement led him to range them from high at both ends to small in the middle. He bracketed them between a tea-caddy and a box of his father's car tools so that none could escape. Then he spread them out again, like playing cards.

Summer was ending. It seemed as if it always was. He had a bike, but Friday night was too much of a treat to go out. He also thought it a squander of precious daylight on his parents' part that they should have been in the pub for an hour before it got dark. And yet, as soon as the outside walls and chimney pots were no longer clear, he swung the curtains decisively together, pushing away what little of the day was left. Once it was going, he wanted to be shut of it. He switched on glowing light that made the living room a secret cave no one could get into.

His parents were used to his daft adoration of books, but for anyone beyond the family to witness his vital playthings would make him blush with shame. Aunts, cousins and uncles would mock him, but what else could you expect? If it hadn't been that, they'd have teased him for something else. They had never actually seen his books, though they had been laughingly told about them by his parents. Books and the people he knew didn't belong together, and that was a fact, but he knew it was impossible to live without either.

He wondered what other eyes had slid across these pages. Their faces could be frightening, or happy. They had come in out of the rain after doing a murder. Or they closed a book and put it down so as to go out and do a good deed. How did you know? You never did. You had to make it all up and scare yourself daft.

In any case, how had they felt about what they were reading? What houses had they lived in, and what sort of schools had they gone to? Did they like their furniture? Did they hate their children? He would rather have been any one of those people than himself. Maybe nobody had read the books. They got them as presents, or bought them and forgot to read them. The thought made him feel desolate, though not for long. Books always took his mind off the world around. He lifted the picture-album of France, and pondered on every voyage the book had made. It had been to Chile and China, and all the other places he could think of, between leaving the printers' and reaching his table in Radford.

A clatter of footsteps at the yardend and the boisterous notes of a voice he did not at first recognise dragged him clear. Print had hooks, but they were made of rubber. Before the warning click of the gatelatch his dozen volumes were scooped off the table and stacked on the floor behind the far side of the dresser.

By the time the door opened the gas was lit and a full kettle set on it. He put sugar, milk and a bottle of coffee on the table, then sat looking through a car magazine as if he hadn't moved all evening. His cousin Raymond was first in the room. No stranger, after all. His mother and father breathed a strong smell of ale.

'He's the quickest lad I know at getting that kettle on the burning feathers!' his father said. 'A real marvel at it. I drove like a demon back from the Crown for my cup o' coffee.'

'And you nearly hit that van coming out of Triumph Road,' Raymond laughed.

Martin wondered whether he should take such praise as it was intended, or hate his father for imagining that he needed it, or despise him for thinking he could get round him in such a way. He was already taller than his father, and there were times when he couldn't believe it, and occasions when he didn't like it, though he knew he had to get used to it. So had his father, but he didn't seem bothered by such a thing. He decided to ignore the praise, though he *had* got the kettle on in record time.

'You brought him up right,' Raymond hung his jacket on the back of the door. 'He worn't drug up, like me.' He bumped into his aunt: 'Oops, duck, mind yer back, yer belly's in danger!'

Martin laughed, without knowing whether he wanted to or not. His father would put up with anything from Raymond, who had been to Approved School, Detention Centre and Borstal, though he was now an honest man of twenty-two, and able to charm anybody when he wanted. He did it so well that you were convinced he would never get caught stealing again. He could also use a bullying, jocular sort of self-confidence, having learned how to live rough, half-inch a thing or two, and die young if he must, without getting sent down every year for a Christmas box or birthday present. Another lesson well taken was that he must always look smart, talk clear and act quick, so that anyone who mattered would think he could be trusted. At Borstal he had done boxing, because it seemed that both God and the Governor were on the side of those who stored the deadliest punch. He had developed one as fast as

179

he could, and wasn't afraid to use it whenever necessary. He was loyal to his family, helping them with money and goods to the best of his ability and hard work. He was often heard to say that he couldn't go back to his old ways, for his mother's sake.

Martin wanted to be like his cousin, though sensing that he might never be so made him look up to him even more. He was certainly glad he'd got the books out of sight before he came in.

Raymond, with his bread and cheese, and cup of coffee, was the first to sit down. Martin moved across the room, leaving the fire to the grown-ups. The yellow flames blazed for them alone, and for their talk that came from the big world of boozers that he hadn't yet entered but was avid to. Raymond stretched out a leg, and expertly belched the words: 'Pardon me!' – at which they all laughed.

He held his cup for more coffee. 'I'll be off to Alfreton again in the morning. Help to build another mile o' that motorway. You know how it's done, don't you? I open my big gob wide. Somebody shovels tar and concrete in. Then I walk along shitting out motorway and coughing up signposts!'

'It'll soon be as far as Leeds, wain't it?' his father said quickly, trying to head off such remarks, which he found a bit too loud-mouthed.

Raymond detected the manoeuvre, and to save face, turned censorious: 'It would be, Joe, if everybody got cracking at their job. But they're too busy looting to get much done. The fields for miles on either side are laid waste by plundering navvies. Some of 'em sit around smoking and talking, and waiting for a turnip to show itself above the soil. As soon as it does, up it comes! They go straight into their snapsacks.'

He was a joker. They weren't sure whether it was true or not. No gaffer could afford to let you get away with not working full-tilt. But he *had* brought vegetables home. Ripping up a basketful was the work of a few minutes in the dusk: 'A bloke the other day come to wok in his minivan,' Raymond told them, 'and drove it a little way into the wood. He kept the engine running so's we wouldn't hear his chain-saw, but when I went in for a piss I saw the bleeder stacking logs in the back. A nice young pine tree had gone, and he covered the stump up wi' leaves. Nowt's safe. It's bleddy marvellous. He's going to get caught one day, doing it in the firm's time!'

Martin seemed born to listen. Maybe it went with collecting books. If he read them properly he'd perhaps start talking a bit more, and it might be easier then to know what other people were thinking.

'He don't say much,' Raymond observed, 'our Martin don't, does he?'

But he did at school. Among his pals he was as bright as an Amazon parrot. If he tackled a book properly, on the other hand, he might talk even less. It was hard to say until he did. Cut anybody's finger off who got too fresh. The teacher once stopped him bashing up another boy, and said if he caught him at it again he'd pull his arm off. He couldn't really be like Raymond, who'd once got chucked out of school for hitting a teacher right between the eyes.

'He'll be at work next year,' his mother nodded at Martin. 'It's looney to keep 'em till they're fifteen, big kids like him. Give him summat to do. *And* bring us some money in.'

'The bloody road tax is twenty-five quid now,' his father said bitterly, and Martin felt as if he were being blamed for it.

'I didn't have one for six months last year,' Raymond boasted. 'I stuck an old Guinness label on the windscreen. Nobody twigged it.'

Martin knew it wasn't true.

'You never did!' his father said, who believed it. 'I wish I'd had such an idea.'

'No, I tell a lie. It was only on for a fortnight. Then I got the wind up, and brought a real 'un.' He turned his grey eyes on to Martin, as if embarrassed by somebody who didn't continually give themselves away in speech. 'I'll get our Martin a job wi' me on the motorway, though,' he said. 'That'll settle his hash. He'll come home every night absolutely knackered.'

I expect I might, Martin thought. 'What would I do?'

'You'd have to get up early, for a start.'

That wouldn't bother him. Lots of people did. 'What time's that?'

'Six.'

'He's dead to the wide at six. It's all I can do to get him out of bed by eight o'clock.'

'I'm not, our mam.'

Raymond looked at the fire, as if he would have spat at the bars if it had been in his own home. 'I pass here in my car at half past. I'll pick you up tomorrow, if you like.'

'Will yer be fit for it?' his father wanted to know.

Martin, taking more coffee and another slice of bread, didn't think he'd heard right. He often looked at the opening of a book, and when he understood every word, couldn't believe he'd read it properly, and then went back to make sure. 'Tomorrow?'

'Well, I din't say owt about yesterday, did I?'

If Raymond said something, he meant it. He often said that you must regret nothing, and that you should always keep promises. It helped his reputation of being a man who showed up in a crowd. So he promised something in a loud voice now and again in order to keep himself up to scratch. 'I'll stop my owd banger outside the Co-op. If you're there I'll take you. If you ain't, I'll just push on.'

'I'll be waiting.' Martin felt like one of those sailors in the olden days who, about to set off west, wasn't sure he would ever get back again.

The sky was clear and cold. He saw it over the house-tops, and above the façade of the bingo hall that he first went into as a cinema one Saturday afternoon nearly ten years ago.

The wet road looked as clean as if a light shone on it. He buttoned the jacket over his shirt. You never wore a top coat to work unless you were one of the older men. It was too early for traffic, making the road look different to when it was pounded by buses and lorries during the day. His mother had disturbed him from a hundred feet under the sand below the deepest part of the ocean when she had tried to wake him. She had to grab the clothes off him in the end.

Sandwiches bulged in his pocket. He enjoyed waiting, but his hands were cold. 'Never put your hands in your pockets when you're on the job,' Raymond had said. 'A lot of 'em do, but it don't look good.' He couldn't do it while waiting to go there, either. He wished he were setting off to work properly, and that he didn't have another year to do before he got real wages. There wasn't much point in starting work today, and then next year as well.

A postman went by on a bike. 'Morning, kid.'

'Morning.'

Raymond's car had rust along the bottom of the door as it swung open towards him. 'Get in.'

He sounded disappointed that Martin had been able to meet him. The car sailed up Wollaton Road like an aeroplane, spun around the traffic island by the Crown, and went along Western Boulevard. 'Tired?'

'It's a treat, being up early.'

'Bring owt t'eat?'

'Yeh. Mam forgot some tea, though.'

'I've got a mashing.' He played the car with hands and feet as if on a big picture-house organ. 'Sugar, tea, and tinned milk – solid like a cannon ball. Enough for a battalion. Trust our mam. She's old-fashioned, but she's a marvel all the same. You can stand a garden fork in *her* strong tea!'

Beyond the town there was a cloud like a big white dog. Martin yawned, and expected it to do the same.

'We like to start as soon as daylight hits,' Raymond went on. 'That's where the money is, in overtime. You don't mind getting out o' yer warm bed when you can mek a bit of money. I'd wok all hours God sends, for money. Watch the tax, though. Bastards will skin you dry, and fry you rotten. Dangerous work, as well. Nearly got scooped up by a mechanical digger the other day. But it's money that I like to be getting into my pocket, fartin' Martin! As soon as I know there's money to be earned I'd dig that soil up with my fingernails. They don't need to tell *me* when to start sweating!'

Martin had a question. 'What do you do with it?'

'Wi' what?'

'The money you get.'

'Ah! Booze a bit – that's me. Treat everybody – now and again. Save a lot, though. Gonna buy a house when I've got the deposit. Me and mam'll live in it. Not the other spongers, though. They wain't get a look in.'

His brothers and sisters had reputations as scroungers. Serve 'em right if Raymond dealt with them as they deserved.

The narrow lane was so rutted he thought they'd get stuck, the car swaying from side to side, sharp privet branches scraping the window. The wheels skidded on the mud in a couple of places, but it didn't bother Raymond. He steered as if in a rally car, then grumbled: 'Fuckers should have cut that hedge down' – seeing in his mirror another car grinding too closely behind.

As they topped the rise tears of muddy water lashed against the windscreen. When the wipers flushed over it Martin saw the vast clayey cutting between green banks. It was a man-made valley occupied by lorries, cranes, mechanical diggers. Those already moving seemed to be the ones that owned it. He was surprised at how few men there were, having expected to see them swarming all over the place.

Raymond drove parallel to the valley, and parked his car by a cluster of huts. He got out, and farted, then stretched his arms and legs. 'See that trailer?'

'Yes.'

'Well, I'm going to book myself in.'

The nearest wooden hut, full of tools, smelt as if it were made of still-growing trees. He expected to tread on leaves as he went in to have a look, but there was a crunch of gravel under his boots. His eyes were sore from little sleep. He yawned while trying to stretch his arms without being seen.

The sound of engines moaned and jerked from the canyon. They formed a chorus. There was never silence. Raw earth was being cleared. Soon it would be covered, and packed, and solidified, and paved to take traffic and huge lorries between London and Leeds. The men who did it knew what their work was for. They could see it as plain as a streak of paint across a piece of new wood. But it must go so slowly that a month was like a day.

Raymond came back wearing a helmet and a livid pink jacket. 'Don't stand idle,' he called sharply, so that Martin didn't know whether he was joking or not. 'Let's get on that motor.'

The dumper truck swayed as it went down the track hewn in the incline. The narrow ledge frightened him, for the dumper might tumble any minute

185

and take both of them to the bottom. Raymond fought with the wheel and gears, laughed and swore as he swung it zig-zag along.

'This fucking thing – it's like a dog: I tamed it a long while ago, so you've no need to worry.' The machine went more quickly. 'If we don't get down in one piece, though, I'll get the push. That's the sort of world we're living in, Martin. Owt happens to this dumper, and I get my cards. Don't matter about us, if we get killed. We'll get compo, but what good does that do yer?'

He drove the petrol-smelling truck under the digger to take its load, then lumbered it back up the escarpment in such a way that Martin didn't think he'd tamed it at all. Tipping it from above helped to heighten the embankment: 'The bleeding gaffer wanted to know what *you* was doing here, so I told him you was the new mash-lad from Cresswell. He's got so much on his plate though, that gaffer, that he don't know whether he's coming or going. Looked a bit gone-out at me, burree din't say owt.'

After two trips Martin decided to stay on top. He could watch the beetling dumpers doing their work from a distance, which was better than being down among them. He remembered a word from school that would describe the long deep scar: geology, geological. The layers of gravel and grit and clay were being sliced like a cake so that the motorway could be pushed through into Yorkshire.

In a while he sat down. It was a struggle to keep the eyes open when you weren't thinking about anything. The wind died and the sun came out. He was dozing in its warm beams, then dreaming, but he never cut off from the distant punch and rumble of machinery, and the occasional shouting that broke through as if finding him at the end of a long search.

Diesel smoke wafted across. He opened his eyes so

as not to lose contact with the sort of work he hoped
to be getting paid for next year. Raymond nudged
him awake: 'You poor bogger! A bit too early in the
morning, was it?'

'No, it worn't,' he snapped.

'You know why, though, don't you?' He had a can
of hot tea, and offered him the lid as a cup. 'Take
this. I'll get some scoff.'

'Why?' The sweet strong tea went straight to the
waking-up box behind his eyes.

'You stayed up too late. Can't go to work early if
you don't get to your wanking pit on time. Not
unless you're over eighteen, anyway. You'll 'ave to
stop reading all them books. Send you blind.'

He'd heard that before – often. 'I'm not tired.'

Raymond rolled a neat cigarette. 'What about some
snout, then?'

'No, thanks.'

He laughed. Smoke drifted from his open mouth.
'That's right. Keep off the fags. Don't booze, either,
or go with women. Stick to your books as long as you
can. And you know why? I'll tell yer: because fags
pack your lungs in, booze softens your brain, and
women give you the clap.'

With that, he went back to work.

Martin didn't know what to make of such advice,
so it didn't seem important. He wished he had one of
the books he'd stacked and shifted about on the table
last night, even if it was only the Bible in Polish, or
the Italian dictionary. When dumper trucks again
moved into the canyon, and the first one came back
loaded, they didn't interest him any more, though he
thought they might if he sat at the wheel of one like
Raymond.

An hour later he was so bored that he felt hungry,
so finished off his last cheese sandwich. Sitting high
up and set apart gave him a picture-view. Nothing
happened, and he was bored, yet everything moved

so slowly that he wouldn't forget it as long as he lived.

Raymond's truck was easy to recognise. He saw clearly across the whole distance, and watched him go with his load up the far slope of the motorway. A wind blew from the streets of a town on the skyline, as if someone on the church top in the middle were wafting it over. With his vivid sight he saw Raymond's truck go behind a long low spoil bank, the helmet moving slowly. Then his body reappeared, and finally the truck again.

It was manoeuvred into a clearing for about the twentieth time, and guided close to the escarpment by another man. It waited a few seconds, as if to get breath, then it tipped its load. There was no pause before setting off quickly towards the excavation for another.

He stared more closely, imagining he was Raymond sitting on the truck and working the levers, confidently steering after four years' experience, smelling old oil and new soil and wondering how much he would coin that day. He wouldn't mind working here, even if he did have to start by seeing to the men's tea and running errands from one hut to another. A mash-lad was better than a school-kid.

The truck reversed towards the precipice at a normal and careful speed. At dusk they'd drive back to Nottingham. Maybe Raymond would call at home for a bite to eat before going to where he lived in the Meadows – though it wasn't likely because he never went visiting in his working clothes.

He could almost hear the engines speeding up. 'I'll get this one over with,' Raymond might be saying, 'then I'll pack it in and piss off out of it. Done enough graft for one day.' He sensed the words going through his brain. He said them aloud, as if to save his cousin the thought or energy.

He couldn't say who was tired most: him, Ray-

mond, or the man whom Raymond's dumper truck
knocked flying over the almost sheer slope. The man
had sauntered out of the way as usual but then, for a
reason which was hard to make out (though he was
sure there must have been one, since there always
was a reason – for everything), he leapt back against
the truck as if to dive underneath.

It wasn't easy to decide the exact point of impact.
The man's spade turned in the air, and Martin swore
he heard the clatter as its metal head caught the side
of the truck.

The body rolled down the steep bank and smashed
into a mechanical digger. He watched Raymond
jump from his seat. Other men lined the top of the
spoil heap. Two or three, Raymond clearly among
them, started to scramble down.

The whole heart-side of Martin's body was dulled
with pain. It lasted a few seconds, then left him
feeling cold, wind-blown and gritty at the eyes, which
now seemed to lose their vision. The sound of an
ambulance came from far away as he walked towards
the huts. His legs and arms shivered as if from
cold. He gripped himself till it stopped. The flashing
blue lights of a police car bobbed along the hedge-
top.

He noticed how pale Raymond was when he got into
the car an hour after his usual knocking-off time. He
smoked a cigarette, something he said he never did
when driving. 'That pig-copper told me I'd killed 'im
on purpose,' he shouted above the engine as it
roared and sent the car skidding along the muddy
lane. 'They said I must have been larking about.'

'I didn't see yer, and I was watching.'

'A few others was as well, so I'm all right for
witnesses. But can you believe it? Killed 'im on
purpose! One of the blokes I'd known for weeks! Can
you imagine him asking a thing like that? Must be

rotten to the bloody core. He just jumped in front of my truck.'

Martin felt as if he was asking the only question in his life that needed a proper answer:

'Why did he do it?'

After half a minute's silence, which seemed so long that Martin thought his cousin would never speak again, unless to tell him to mind his own business, Raymond said: 'You won't guess. Nobody on this earth would. I'll tell yer, though. He dropped his packet o' fags in front of my truck, and because he thought the wheels would crush 'em, he jumped to pick 'em up. The daft bastard didn't want to lose his fags. Would you believe it? Didn't *think*! Blokes who don't think deserve all they get. I'd have given him half of my own fags though, if only he'd left 'em alone.' He smiled bleakly at his untested generosity. 'Can't understand him doing a thing like that. I thought I knew him, but bogger me if I did. You don't know anybody, *ever*, Martin. So never think you do.'

'He's dead now, though.'

'The daft bleeder.'

Martin said he was sorry it happened. He hated feeling the tears at his eyes as sharp as glass. 'Who was he?'

'An old chap, about forty-odd. Happy old chokker. He was allus singing, he was. You could tell from his mouth, but nobody ever *heard* him because of the engines kicking up such a noise. He didn't sing when he thought we could hear him. Funny bloke altogether. All my life I've been careful, though, that's the best on it. I never wanted that to happen. I'm not a murderer, it don't matter what that copper tried to say. "I'm not a murderer, your honour! Honest, I'm not!" That's what I'll shout out in court when the case comes up.'

Back in the lighted streets, Martin said nothing. He

agreed on his cunning, for he caught the landlord at a time when he was unable to imagine such an occurrence, which allowed the old man to get in some minutes of tap-dance and sing-song before the night was brought to an end.

As he waited by the dregs of a second pint, his free hand began to shake, and his slate-grey eyes took on such a glitter that it seemed unlikely they provided him with much visibility. He drew his sleeve across his mouth to wipe the beer away, but also to erase any tremble that might betray his intention, suggesting a strength of character from former days that had not yet totally vanished. He blinked nervously and, when his arm came down, his tongue darted twice across his lips. He wore a knotted tie over a white collar that turned up at the ends, and it could be seen that his dark grey jacket and trousers didn't quite match.

In the general astonishment at the clattering dance everyone looked at his shoes rather than his face, sensing that if a collapse were to come it would begin with them, and they would see the full drama from the start. Yet the face was more interesting if only because it was difficult to fix on, and hard to accept what it was saying to those who thought only to observe the feet. Anyone who did look at his lips might realise he was trying to tell them something.

His hands were held flat in front as if to push off his audience should they try and drag him down – as he expected and dared them to. They hardly heard the tapping of his feet, and few made out the tune he was singing, for the pub was far from quiet. His mouth moved to a definite song but the words were hard to catch. He relived the murder, but no one listened to his gospel-truth. His sneer was like spit in their eyes though they did no more than grin, or call to get his knees up, or ask him to remember his age and not be such a loon. Or they ignored him while supping their final jars.

He would dance while he could, and tell again what he'd whispered in that shell-hole near Gommecourt fifty years ago. He shouted names and phrases, and sometimes made them rhyme, till a few listened, though heard little that made sense. He tapped the rhythm and told it clear, and wondered when they'd pull him down and ask why he'd never been taken to the cop-shop and relieved of his money, belt, braces, shoes and false teeth, and got thrown into a stone cell, and brought into court (where he'd have said nothing from start to finish), and finally taken into the hangman's yard as a proper end to a wickedness he hadn't repeated to a soul till an age when the edge of his younger days came back and time had no meaning because there wasn't much of it left.

Every stone had beetles underneath. They lay still and quiet, because of all creatures on earth they were good at knowing how, but in the last few months they'd been growing bigger, till he felt the boulder ready to surge into the air and crush him to even less than a beetle when it came down. The crime had kept him loving and industrious ever after, and even now God hadn't paid him out.

Nevill passed the house of a blacksmith's noisy family. The up-and-down stretch of common known as the Cherry Orchard was blocked from the west by Robins Wood. The sun glowed on a bed of clouds, and the surrounding grass appeared so green from his place of hiding that it seemed as if a secret kingdom shone from under the ground.

Too far off to be noticeable, Nevill saw the man walking towards the wood – having been daft enough to think that secrets could be kept. Silence increased the quality of the glow. The stark side of the trees stood out as if they would melt, part of the most perfect summer since the fourteen year old century had turned.

Nevill watched Amy follow her fancyman from the lane, by which time he was already waiting in the wood. He plucked a juicy grass stem and, now that they were out of sight, moved along a depression – in case they should be looking from the bushes – towards the spot a hundred yards above where they had entered.

A breeze which carried the smell of grass made him hungry. He had come out before his tea, tracking to where he thought she had gone. There had to be a day when he came home early. The farmer he worked for lent him a gun so that he could stalk hares and be sure of hitting them. He moved like a tree that seemed always in the same place to the delicate senses of a rabbit. Then he took five minutes to lift his gun so that they didn't stand a chance. Even so, one sometimes escaped in a last-minute zig-zag too quick to be sighted on. Because the farmer gave only one cartridge at a time he could afford no waste. A big rabbit lasted two meals, and made a smell for any man to come home to.

The last of the sun flushed white and pink against his eyes. A raven circling over the wood told him they were still there, and hadn't gone out the other side towards the west. Its black gloss turned purple in the evening light.

Kneeling, he wondered whether or not to go back to the house and leave them alone. Now that he knew for certain, there seemed no point in pursuing them, for he could call the tune any time he liked. But his legs wouldn't stop his slow encroachment on that part of the wood they had gone into. A cloud of gnats pestered him. If he had been walking at a normal pace he could have reached home and forgotten all about it, but the deliberate putting forward on to the grass of one foot after another was as if he advanced on a magnetised track impossible to side-step.

Shadows aggrandised each tree and solitary bush. Two rabbits ran from the wood. One stared at him, then sat up and rubbed its paws, while the other turned away with its white tail shivering in the breeze. He heard a hooter from Wollaton colliery, and the blink of his left eyelid wasn't sufficient to warn the rabbits, one of which was big enough for the pot.

Fingers itched for the safety catch, the shotgun lifting inch by inch. One would be dead for sure, but he fought his instinct, staying the gun while in the grip of something firmer. Rabbits swarmed so much this summer that a week ago he caught two with one bullet.

The long dusk began. A platoon of starlings scoured back and forth on a patch of grass to leave no worm's hiding place unturned. He wanted to light his pipe and smoke off the gnats, but any movement might reveal his place, so he became a flesh statue with head bowed, green jacket blending into green.

The crack of twigs sounded and she walked, without turning left or right, straight across the Cherry Orchard and back towards the lane. It wasn't the nearest way home but, when close to the house, she'd expect him to see her coming from the Woodhouse direction in which her mother lived. He smiled at such barefaced cunning, in which they'd talked up their little plot together, he deciding to stay another ten minutes in the wood after she had got clear of it.

Nevill needed only a few paces to reach the trees. Dodging the brambles, he walked from the thigh, toes and balls of the feet descending so as to avoid the heel on unseen twigs. He heard the stream that ran down the middle of the narrow wood. Blackberries were big and ripe. A pigeon rattled up, and he made towards its noise, advancing at the crouch, knowing every patch because his cottage was on the northern tip. When a match scraped along a box he stiffened.

The odour of fungus and running water on clean pebbles was sharpened by the cool of the evening. It wasn't quite dusk, but Nevill had to peer so as not to mistake him for the shadow of a bush. Looking for the first star, he lowered his head before finding one. The sky was still pale blue.

He saw him by the stream smoking a cigarette. A loosened tie hung around his neck, and he irritatedly brushed leaves from the legs of his dark suit. He whistled the bars of a tune, but suddenly stopped, as if not wanting to hear anything that would take him so far from what had just passed between him and Amy.

Nevill lifted the gun, butt-first. When a frog plopped into a side arm of the stream he saw the rings, and the man turned sharply at the noise as he decided it was time to get out of the wood. After two paces a shadow came at his head which had the force of the world concealed in it. An electric light went on for a second and revealed the trees roundabout. Often when a rabbit wouldn't die he battered the neck, and his rage was so great that it was no more difficult to smash the man's temple while he lay on the ground. There was a smell of hard drink when he knelt to make sure he was dead.

At the edge of the wood dusk was coming across the Cherry Orchard like a scarf. When Nevill fired, a rabbit spun on the ground. Then he fastened its two back legs together and walked towards the darker part of the common.

Standing at the door to look for him Amy heard the shot softened like a thunderclap in the distance, and shivered at the evening chill. Nevill passed by the blacksmith's house and went down the lane, under

the long railway bridge to Lottie Weightman's beer-
off in the village. He sold his rabbit for sixpence, then
drank a pint. They were talking about the war, of how
everybody was going, some saying what damned
fools they were, while others thought it the only
thing to do. He sat observing them with his slate-
grey eyes, smiling at their expressions that did not
seem to know what life was about.

Next day he went back into the wood and, hanging
his jacket from the spike of a dead branch, hauled the
body from its hiding place. He scraped off the turf
and hacked at the roots. The soil was dry, but
moistened lower down. With Amy last night he had
lain back to back, thinking he'd never touch her
again. Each press of the spade, pull at the handle and
lift, reinforced his feelings about her. From the clear
land of the Cherry Orchard he heard children, so put
his jacket on and went swiftly to the edge of the
wood.

'You can't come in 'ere.'

They were three ragged-arsed kids from Radford.
'We on'y want blackberries.'

'It's private.'

They grumbled.

'Gerroff – or you'll get a good-hiding.'

He looked as if he'd do it, so they went, though
one of them called from a distance and before fleeing
'Fuckin' owd bastard!'

He worked more quickly and, when the neat
oblong hole was deep enough, heard the body
thump to the bottom. The smashed head vanished
under a first curtain of soil. Dead twigs and leaf-
mould disguised the grave. He leaned against a tree
to smoke his pipe, till sweat subsided and his breath
came back, then he walked through the deepest
grass to get the soil off his boots, for it wouldn't do to
be untidy if you were going into town.

Walking up the hill towards Canning Circus he

met others on the same errand. He spat on both hands for luck and rubbed his palms on hearing the clash of a band outside the drill hall, thinking that the army would be as good a place to hide as any.

The smell from his skin went as quickly as the spit dried. After passing the medical and getting his shilling he drank a pint in the canteen. Two hours later and still in their own clothes they were marched back down Derby Road to tents on Wollaton Park – only a mile from the wood where the fresh body lay buried.

Farmer Taylor could keep his job at fifteen bob a week. With two hours off the next day, he called to say he had packed it in, and expected to be turned out of his cottage, but the farmer smiled: 'I knew you would. I told you he'd be the first to go. Didn't I tell you, Martha? You wait, I said, he'll go, Nevill will! I'll lose a good man, but I know he'll go. Wish I could be in the old regiment myself. I know of no finer thing than going to fight for your country.'

There wasn't much need to talk. He was invited into the parlour and given a mug of ale.

'You'll mek a fine sowjer,' Taylor went on. 'I expected no less. Come and see us when you've got your khaki on.' He gave him a florin above his wages: 'Your wife can stay in the cottage. I'll see nowt happens to her.'

'I expect she'll be able to look after herself,' Nevill said cheerfully.

The farmer gave him a hard look: 'Ay, you'll mek a fine sowjer. Your sort allus do.'

He went home: 'I've gone and enlisted. You can carry on all you like now, because I won't be coming back.'

She gave him some bread and cheese. 'God will pay you out, leaving me like this.'

He wanted to laugh. When she went on the prowl for her man it wouldn't do her much good. He went upstairs to change into his best suit. The small room with its chest of drawers and flowered paper was part of them, as was the bed with its pillows and counterpane. She kept the house like a new pin, he had to admit, but it made no difference. He tied his working clothes and spare boots into a parcel, and pushed it under the bed with his toe-cap. He wouldn't be back for any of them. Most other men in camp wore their oldest clothes, some nearly in rags, but he wanted to look smart even before the khaki came. If they took him away to be hanged he didn't want to take the drop looking like a scarecrow.

He stood in the doorway for a last look at the kitchen. 'Everybody's rushing to the colours.'

'More fool them. It doesn't mean you've got to join up as well. You're nearly thirty: let the young mad-'eads go.'

He didn't know what she had to cry for. She should be glad to get shut of him. He put two sovereigns between the pot cats on the shelf: 'Don't lose 'em.'

When she took off her pinafore and began to fold it he was frightened at having taken the King's shilling. One thing led to another when you killed somebody. Birds were whistling outside the open window. She'd hung the mats on the line. In his weakness he wanted to sit down, but knew he mustn't.

She rushed across to him. He lost his stiffness after a few moments, and held her. They had been married in Wollaton church five years ago, but when they went upstairs he felt that he hadn't known her till now.

He forgot her grey eyes and her auburn hair when walking back by the dark side of the wood. If God paid him out it would be because God was a German bullet. As for the bloke whose brains he had knocked in, it served him right. He was tempted to dig by the bush and look at the body, to make sure everything wasn't happening in the middle of a dream, but he didn't have a spade.

The day was rotting. He breathed dusk through his nostrils, a smell that was enough to turn you as balmy as a hayfork, especially in such silence before rain. Happiness made him walk upright across the Cherry Orchard without looking back.

'You'll dig yourselves ten feet under,' the sergeant shouted, 'when the first shell bursts.'

On parade he was ordered to tie a white tape on his arm, the mark of a lance-corporal, till uniforms came and he could sew on the proper stripe. He was a more promising soldier than the rest, for he did not live from day to day like most of the platoon, nor even from hour to hour as some of them cared to. He existed by the minute because every one contained the possibility of him being taken off and hanged. The grave was a deep one, and the man not known in the district – he reasoned hopefully while lying in the bell tent with eleven others and listening to rain-drops hitting the canvas. It was also a time when scores of thousands were going to other towns to get into their favourite regiments, so maybe no one would even look for him.

During every package of sixty seconds he gave absolute attention to the least detail of military routine, and became the keenest man in the platoon. When rifles were issued he was careful that each round reached a bull's eye. The sling was firm around his arm and shoulder, body relaxed, feet splayed, and eye clear at the sights.

Every battalion had its snipers. 'On a dark night a lighted match can be seen nine hundred yards away,' they were told, 'and that's as far as from the Guild-hall to the bloody Castle!'

It was also the distance from here to where *he* was buried, Nevill thought.

'Pay attention, or I'll knock your damned 'ead off!'

The sergeant savvied any mind that wandered, and Nevill knew he mustn't be caught out again.

He slid into the loop-holed sniper's post built by the sappers in darkness. Sacking was around his head, and mud-coloured tape swathed his rifle. He looked slowly from left to right, towards wire and sandbags across ground he had been over in darkness and seen in daylight through a periscope. He knew each grass-clump and crater. A faint haze hovered. Smells of cooking and tobacco drifted on the wind. He savoured the difference between a Woodbine and a Berlin cigar, till a whine and a windrush eruption of chalk and soil caused his elbow to tremble at a shell dropping somewhere to the left. The camouflage net shivered. He heard talking in the trenches behind. An aeroplane flew high.

Amy worked on filling shells at Chilwell factory, earning three times the amount he got as a corporal marksman, but he sent half his pay for her to put in a bank, though he didn't expect ever to get home and claim it because either a bullet or a rope (or a shell) was sure to pay him out. I always loved *you*, and always shall, she wrote. Aye, I know, same here, he answered – but not telling what he knew, and cutting her from his mind in case he got careless and was shot. He smiled at the justice of it.

In the space between one minute and the next he expected to see a party of men coming to get him for the hangman's yard whose walls would smell like cold pumice and rotting planks. He was ready for it to happen from any direction he could name, so that even in the débris of the trenches there was no one smarter at spotting misdemeanours in his own men, or fatal miscalculations on the enemy parapet.

A machine gun half a mile away stitched thoughts

back into his brain, eyes turning, head in a motion
that scanned the faint humps of the broken line. He
didn't want to give up his perfected system of counting the minutes which kept him going in a job that
held little prospect of a long life. All snipers went
west sooner or later. He was glad that whole days
passed without thinking of Amy, because she took
his mind off things.

A smudge of grey by a sandbag, and then a face,
and he lined up the sights instantly and pressed the
trigger. The crack travelled left and right as he reloaded almost without movement, the bolt sliding
comfortably in. The bullet took half a second to reach
the face that had sprung back. He heard the word for
stretcher bearer – *krankentrager* – and wanted to
laugh because, as in a game of darts or cribbage, he
had *scored*. The more he killed, the less chance
there'd be of getting called to account. He didn't
want to know more than that. It was dangerous to
think. You're not here to think but to do as you're
effing-well told – and never you forget it or by God
I'll have your guts for garters and strangle you to
death with 'em. But they didn't need to roar such
rules at him.

A retaliating machine gun opened from three
hundred yards left. He saw the gunner. Chalk that
jumped along was nowhere close enough. An itching started on his cheek, and an impulse to scratch
was fought down. When it came back he turned
his body cold. It was an almost pleasurable irri-
tation that couldn't be ignored, but he resisted it,
minute by minute. You had only to be at the Front for
an hour and you were as lousy as if you'd been there
ten years.

Last week he'd had a fever, and hadn't been able
to do his work. No sniper was allowed out with a
fever or a cold. With a fever you shook, and with a
cold you dozed – though a true sniper would forget

such things in his moment of action. Yet an experienced sniper was too valuable to waste. He sensed as much when he moved along the communication trenches at dawn or dusk, and observed how the officers looked at him – after their first curiosity at seeing such an unusual specimen – as if he were a man singled out for a life even worse than death, cooped up like a rat that only waited its turn to kill without fair fight. He knew quite plainly that many didn't like him because sniping was a dirty weapon like poison gas or liquid fire.

The trench was disturbed. Every eye fixed his stretch of land. They looked but did not see. He let his body into complete repose so as to make no move. The range card was etched on to his brain, and his eyes caught all activity, had even sharper vision because of the body's helplessness. The whole view was exposed to his basic cunning. His itching leg was forgotten when he pressed the trigger and killed the machine gunner.

Out of the opposite trench, a few fingers to the right, came a man who stood on the sandbags and beckoned. He wore a dark suit. A tie was unfastened around his neck. He bent down to brush chalk-grit from his trousers. When he straightened himself, he smiled.

Nevill lay in the water of his sweat, his teeth grinding as if to take a bite out of his own mouth. His body wasn't dead, after all. The man was afraid to come closer. Grey clouds formed behind his head, till he became part of them, when Nevill took a long shot almost in enfilade, and brought down a man who looked up from the second line of trenches.

If the man had still been alive Nevill would have shouted at him for his foolishness. Mistakes were as common as Woodbines. Even the old hands made them occasionally, as if tired of a caution which wouldn't let them be themselves. Something inside decided, against their will, that they'd had enough. In an unguarded moment their previous carefree nature took over – and they died. He smiled at the thought that no such fecklessness could kill him, no matter how deep down it lay.

He couldn't get out of his place till darkness. Danger time was near. If he chanced one more round they'd get a bearing and smother his place with shot shell and shit. Papier mâché heads painted to look real were put up so that when the sniper's bullet went clean through back and front, a pinpoint bearing could be made between the two holes which would lead with fatal accuracy to him. So when he saw a head tilted slightly forward and wearing no helmet he didn't shoot. If he kept as still as dead they would never see him, and he'd known all his life how to do that. When he played dead he was most alive. He felt like laughing but, knowing how not to, was hard to kill. As if in agreement the earth rumbled for half a minute under another nearby burst of shell. It grew in intensity till it sounded like a train going through Lenton station. He wanted to piss, but would have to keep it in.

Tomorrow he would be in a different position and, corked face invisible, could start all over again. He lay by the minute, sun burning through clouds as if intent on illuminating only him. A shot at dusk might succeed, when the setting sun behind sharpened their line of trenches, but only one, because they would be waiting, and he was too old a hand to get killed just before knocking off time.

Raindrops pestered a tin can, and caused an itch at his wrist. There was better visibility after a shower, though gas from his rifle in the dampened atmosphere might give him away if he fired. Their eyes were as good as his when they decided to look. He felt like a rabbit watching from its burrow, and counted the minutes more carefully. If they found him, he'd die. He craved to smoke his pipe. No sniper was taken prisoner. Nor their machine gunners. He felt cramp in his right foot, but tightened himself till it went.

The minute he woke in the morning, either at rest or on the march, or in the line, his first thought was not to decipher where he was but to realise that he hadn't yet been taken up for the man he had killed. He kissed his own wrist for luck. Other soldiers roundabout wondered why he smiled, while they only scowled or cursed.

Lying in his cramped hole sometimes brought on a faintness from which the only way out was to spread arms and legs as far as they would go, then get into the open and run. He would certainly be killed, so when blood packed at the extremities of hands and feet, thereby thinning at the heart, he called the minutes through and counted them. Sixty minutes made a platoon called an hour. Twenty-four hours formed as near as dammit two battalions of a day. He deployed his platoons and battalions of time and sent them into the soil. A shell once burst too near and he pissed into his rags – but kept his place and his life. When a machine gun peppered around no-man's-land in the hope of catching him, a man from his own trenches stopped the racket with a burst from a Lewis gun.

The minutes he hewed out of life, from the air or his own backbone, or plucked even from the din of the guns, saved him time and time again. In pushing aside the image of the hangman coming to get him across no-man's-land (or waiting in the form of a Provost Marshal's red cap when he went back through the communication trench and up towards the broad light of the day that was to be his last) he had only to punctuate his counting of the minutes by a careful shot at some flicker on the opposite sandbags. Away from the trenches, he could not wait to get back, even if on frontline duty as one of a back-breaking carrying party, or as an enfilading sharp-shooter during a trench raid. But mostly he belonged in a sniper's position that needed only eyes, brain and a steady finger at the trigger while he lay there all day and counted the minutes.

A week in the trenches was as long as a month or a year. He counted the minutes while others marked off the days. But all of them were finally without time and covered in mud, one in ten lost through shellfire, raids, frostbite and bullets.

They drudged to the rear and one night, wet from head to foot, Nevill joined his company in a rush across the churned turf of a field towards the bath-house. Everyone stripped to let the sanitary men get their underclothes. Lice were everywhere. Scabies was common, and spread like chalkdust on a windy day. Some scratched themselves till bloody all over, and were treated with lavish doses of sulphur – which might give them dermatitis if they got too much of it. Nevill endured the terrible itching, even in his sniper's post, but on normal duty he woke himself after a few hours' sleep by a wild clawing at his clothes.

Water gushed from the taps only one point off freezing. They had expected it to be hot, so sounded as if a pack of ravening lions had got loose. The captain, transfixed by their mutinous swearing, hoped the sergeant-major would be along to get them moving into the water no matter how cold it was. Hard to understand their rage when they endured so much agony of life and limb on duty in the trenches. One man slipped on the slatted planks, and cursed the army.

'This is the last straw!' he shouted.

No one laughed, even when he was advised: 'Well, eat it, then.'

Nevill, the icy chute spraying at him, let out a cry that stopped everyone's riotous catcalls: 'Fucking hell, it's too hot! It's scalding me to death. Turn it off! I'm broiled alive. Put some cold in, for Christ's sake!'

They began laughing at the tall thin chap fooling around with knees and knackers jumping up and down, a look of mock terror in the fiery stillness of his eyes and the falling line of his lips.

Once fastened into the separate world of his own outlandish shouts, Nevill went on calling loud and clear: 'My back's on fire! I'm broiling in *hell*! Turn that effing water off, or put some cold in, *please*! This steam's blinding my eyes. Turn it off!'

Others joined in and shouted the magic phrases like a chorus line at the music hall. They no longer hung back, but took to the water without further complaint.

Nevill stopped, and gripped the soap to wash. The muddy grime swilled off, and his face turned red as if steam had really worked the colour-change, not shame. Then he laughed again with the others while they blundered around fighting for the soap.

They collected warm and fumigated underwear. After breakfast came pay parade and later, with francs in their pockets and a few hours' kip behind their eyes, they were away to the estaminet for omelette, chips and wine, where they went on singing Nevill's catch-line: 'Turn that effing water off, or put some cold in please!'

What made him shout those words he didn't know, but the captain marked him for his sergeant's stripe, seeing a priceless N.C.O. who could control his men by firmness – and displays of wit, however crude. Apart from which, there was no better off-hand shot in the battalion, though as a sergeant his sniping days were over.

After a hard week's training for 'the battalion in attack' they went back to the line with buckles, boots and buttons shining. The noise of guns took up every square inch of air around the face, kept a trembling under the feet for days. They said that gunfire brought rain. Cordite gathered full-bellied clouds that emptied on trenches to make all lives a misery. At the best of times a trench was muddy. The common enemy was rain, and the guns that shook soil down.

The few shells from the other side blew the earth walls in, no matter how well-revetted. When Nevill was buried he thought the hangman had come and gone already. He smelled quick-lime. In his tomb, yet knowing where he was, made him wonder if the man had been alive when he had buried him in Robins Wood. But he hadn't gone back till next day, and he'd been dead by then right enough.

Nevill was earthed-in with bullet pouches, water bottle and rifle. In other words – as Private Clifford said, who found him more alive than two others whose names he couldn't remember as soon as they were dead – he was buried with full military honours, and you couldn't want more than that, now could you, sarge?

The pattacake soil-smell was everywhere, and the only thing that saved Nevill was his tin hat which, being strapped firmly on, had enough all-round rim to trap sufficient air for him to breathe till he was pulled free.

Every fibre of skin bone and gristle vibrated to the pounding. Could anything live under it? He drew himself into his private world and remembered how Amy had answered that she had nothing to forgive him for. She was never to realise he'd known about her love affair, though no doubt she wondered still where the chap had hopped it to. Maybe to the Western Front, like the rest of us. And if he hadn't sent a letter, what was funny in that? Nevill felt almost sorry she'd been ditched by two instead of one, though perhaps it wasn't all that rare when so many men had gone away at once.

Yet he needn't have worried about her wellbeing, for she sent him a parcel of tinned jam and biscuits and salmon, and a note saying she was working at Chilwell Depot till as close as she could get to her confinement which, he surmised, couldn't by any stretch of counted minutes be his kid. By earning her own money she could do as she liked, and in any case he had bigger things on his plate than to care what she got up to. 'I expect my missis is having a little bit on the side while I'm away,' he heard Private Jackson say. 'Suppose I would if I was her, damn her eyes!'

Being in a webbing harness of cross-straps and belt, with all appurtenances hanging therefrom, made him feel he no longer belonged to himself, since a devil's hook in any part of his garb could swing him from here to eternity without a by-your-leave. He had a date with some kind of hangman, and that was a fact. The unavoidable settled his gloom, and was only lifted when his duties as platoon sergeant made him forget.

Under the hangings of equipment he was almost skeletal. The other sergeants – when he shared Amy's food parcel – chaffed that a bullet wouldn't find him. But he ate like a wolf, and no flesh grew. He worried, they said. He worked too hard. He was never still. You needn't let a third stripe kill you. The men didn't like him, yet under his eternal fussing felt that he would never let them down.

Drumfire crumbled the walls between compartments of the minutes. A shake entered his limbs that he had seen in others, and which he thought would never afflict him. As a sniper he had gone over after the first rush of infantry, but now there would be no distinction. He'd be in the open without his hide-away. It wasn't the first time, but they'd been trench raids, and not the big attack. He held his hand down, and counted till the trembling stopped.

The guns were finishing off every living thing, and all they had to do was walk across on the day and take over what was left. 'Only, don't scratch your lily-white ankles on the rusty barbed wire, lads. And don't fall into an 'orrible shell-hole. And if you see a hot shell sizzling towards you, just push it to one side with your little finger and tell it to piss off' – he'd heard Robinson diverting his mates the other day. Nobody else thought it would be a walkover, though he supposed a few of the brass hats hoped against hope.

He walked along the trench, lifting his boots through the foot-depth of mud.

'Had yer rum?'

They read his lips in the noise. 'Yes, sergeant.'

'Had yer rum, then?'

'I'm tiddly already, sarge!'

'Answer properly when yer're spoken to.'

There was no doubt about the next one: 'Had yer rum?'

'Yes, sergeant.'

'Wake up then, or you'll be on a charge.'

'Bollocks.'

He swung back. 'If yo' don't have less chelp, Clifford, I'll put yer bollocks where yer fucking 'ead should be.'

The man laughed. 'Sorry, sergeant.'

Live and let live. He moved on. 'Had yer rum?'

'It makes me sleepy, sergeant.'

'You'll wake up in a bit, never bloody fear. Had yer rum?' – and on till he had made sure of everyone.

He stood by a ladder and drank his own, except for a drop in the bottom which he threw into the mud for luck. They called it the velvet claw because it warmed yet ripped your guts. Some couldn't take it, but those who could always drank any that went buck-shee.

He saw that the stars had turned pale. The guns made a noise that two years ago would have torn him apart had it been sprung on him. He pressed his feet together so that his knees wouldn't dance. There'd never been such a week of it. Every minute was hard to drag out. Darkness was full of soil and flashes. The counting melted on his tongue. For a moment he closed his eyes against the roaring light, then snapped them open.

One dread stamped on another. Explosions from guns and Stokes mortars dulled the feel of a greased rope at the neck. His cheeks shook from the blast of a near-miss. With bayonet fixed and day fully light the only way out was over the bags and at the Gerries. The shuddering of his insides threatened to send him into a standing sleep, so he moved up and down the trench to cut himself free of it – and to check every man's equipment. Nothing bore thinking about any more. Under the feet and through the mud a tremor which rocked his temples was connected to a roar in the sky travelling from the south. Another explosion came, and more until the final whistles began. They were letting off the mines before Zero.

Faces to either side were dull and shocked. One or two smiled stupidly. A youth muttered his prayers (or maybe they were curses) and Nevill knew that if he stopped he wouldn't be able to stand up. They were trapped, no matter what they had done. The straight and cobblestoned gas-lit streets of Radford replaced everything with carbide-light clarity. It was a last comforting feel of home, and when it vanished the trap was so final that it seemed impossible ever to get out, though he never lost hope.

Some leaned, or tried to fold themselves, wanting soil for safety. One man was eating it, but blood and flesh and scraps of khaki were up the side of the trench, and his arm was gone. Nevill shouted at them to stand up. He was thrown to one side as pebbles and slabs of chalk spattered his helmet, but he still called hoarsely at them to stand up to it. Screams came from the next bay, and another call for stretcher bearers. Lieutenant Ball examined his luminous watch, and Nevill wondered how much longer they'd be.

Over the parapet he saw flashes in the smoke and mist, an uneven row of bursts where trenches should have been. His watch said seven twenty-five. Amy's letters showed more tenderness than either had felt when they were together. There was more than there would ever be for him should he get back, because it wasn't his baby she was carrying. He won his struggle against her memory by counting each blank minute, knowing there weren't many left before they ascended the swaying ladders.

It was a hard pat at the shoulder that made him turn:

'Yes, sir?'

A company runner stood by. The pale-faced lieutenant of nineteen looked forlorn under his helmet, but regained sufficient competence to tell him: 'You're to go back to Battalion Headquarters, Sergeant Nevill.'

'Now, sir?'

Lieutenant Ball smiled, as if to indicate that such a lunatic signal had nothing to do with him. 'Seems so. You're to go out of the line.'

Nevill gripped his rifle, a vision of himself raising it to the 'on guard' position and bayoneting his officer. The horror of it broke his habit of obedience.

'What for, sir?'

The barrage would lift any second. Lieutenant Ball looked at his watch again, and didn't turn from it till the guns stopped. 'How do I know?'

The hangman would be there, for sure. 'Let me go over, sir. I've waited a long while to have a proper go at them. I can see what they want at Brigade as soon as I come back this afternoon!'

Nevill had fathered the platoon, so it would be vile not to let him take part in the big attack. Silence was filled by the noise of the birds. They were always busy, even when the guns were at it. He stuffed the message into his pocket and said:

'See that you do.'

'Thank you, sir.'

Whistles cut along the crowded slit in the earth, and Nevill shouted them into the open.

Full daylight met them as soon as they were up the ladders. Many clawed their way by planks or soil to gain freedom from the stink, shadows and un-certainty of the trench. Men on either side were falling under loads they could hardly support. High-stepping through their own wire, they went on under the mist as if that too weighed more than they could carry.

Shells of shrapnel balls exploded above their heads. They stopped silently, or rolled against the soil as if thrown by an invisible hand. Or they were hidden in a wreath of smoke and never seen again. The wire was like a wall. The guns had cut only one gap so they were like a football crowd trying to get off the field through a narrow gate on which machine guns were trained.

He sang to himself, wanting to get on. The men walked slowly because they couldn't go back. The biggest paper bags in the world were bursting above their heads. Minutes were unimportant. Every second was a king. He had to see his men through the wire. Lieutenant Ball disappeared as if he'd never existed. When they lagged, Nevill cursed from be-hind. He wanted to run but didn't know whether

front or back would be any good so got ahead to coax
them through bullets and shrapnel:

'Come on, move. Keep your dressing there. Keep
your dressing. Keep moving, lads.'

They couldn't hear, but read his lips if they saw
them, and came on as if they too had been counting
the minutes, and were terrified of some hangman or
other. He wanted them to know that safety lay in
doing as they were told and in getting forward. A
few of his platoon were in advance of the company.
He didn't know where the others had gone. While
still in the German wire more shellbursts caught
them. He was anxiously looking for a way through.
You couldn't hear the birds any more. Machine guns
never stop.

He knelt, and fired towards the parapet, loading
and reloading till he felt a bang at his helmet, and
was pulled as if he were a piece of rope in a tug-o'-
war. If it went on he would snap. In the darkness
someone screamed in one ear when he was drawn
icily apart, and he wondered why there was no light,
thinking maybe they were going to bury him in
Robins Wood, except that he was in France near a
stink-hole called Fonky-bleeding-Villas.

He didn't know who was trying to yank him clear,
but there was a smell of steel that burned so fiercely it
turned blue. He rolled over and over. He opened his
eyes, and took off his waterbottle to drink. The
shrapnel had stunned him but he was unhurt except
for a graze on the scalp.

The man by his side said: 'Not too much, sergeant.
We'll need it for later.'

The stream in Robins Wood ran through his
mouth. He counted the minutes to stop himself
drinking to the bottom. 'Who are yer, anyway?'

'I'm Jack Clifford, sergeant. You know *me*!'

'I was bleddy stunned.' He looked around.
'Where's your rifle?'

'I lost it, sergeant. I don't know.'

'Oh, did yer? You'll be bleddy for-it, then.'

He began to cry.

'Where are yer from?'

'Salisbury Street, sergeant.'

'Got any Mills bombs?'

They were too far off to be any use, but he had.

Pulling off his burden of equipment, and without his helmet, Nevill edged to the rim of the crater. A leg with a boot on it hung over the other lip. He beckoned Clifford to follow, but indicated not too quickly. After a full minute, raising his head, and positioning himself, he fired a whole clip at men on the German parapet. Clifford got higher and threw a grenade, shouting: 'Split this between yer!'

Machine gun bullets swept across. Clifford screamed and rolled back.

Something had struck Nevill's shoulder, and his arm felt as if gripped by an agonising cramp, but with shaking hand he bound both field dressings across Clifford's white and splintered ribs: 'That'll see yer right till we get back. The fuckers are picking us off like rabbits. We don't stand a chance, so we'd better stay where we are.'

'The red caps'll 'ave me. I've lost me rifle,' Clifford said.

Nevill wanted to tell him that it didn't look as if anybody would have him any more, though you couldn't say as much to a young lad. 'Them boggers wain't come for you,' he comforted him. 'It's me they're after. They sent a signal for me.'

'They don't come over the top,' Clifford said, 'do they?' He tried to spit, then seemed to think that if he did he'd die. 'Not them, they don't. If the Gerries didn't shoot 'em, *we* would, wouldn't we, sergeant?'

'Happen we might. Just keep still, and don't worry.'

Blood was pumping like a spring in autumn, but he

knew no tourniquet would hold it. 'Let me tell you summat,' Nevill said, thinking to take his mind off it.

Clifford tried to laugh. 'What, me owd cock?'

'In September, I murdered somebody. Lay still, I said, and don't talk.'

His white face grimaced in agony. 'You're having me on!'

'Before I enlisted, I mean.'

'Got to save our strength. The Gerries'll get us.'

Nevill fought to stop himself fainting. 'No time. I'll tell you about it if you'll listen.' He looked around as if someone else might hear, then pulled Clifford towards him with a desperate grip, shouting into his ear when shells exploded close, and telling his story so that Clifford, behind eyes that stared wildly one minute and were closed the next, couldn't doubt his confession.

A greater truth was choking him, but he forgot to be afraid of machine guns and searching shrapnel while Nevill spoke his deadly tale in which he embroidered the homely Nottingham names to divert Clifford from the agony that would not let him live. He brought in the sound of Woodhouse and Radford, Robins Wood and Wollaton, Lenton and the Cherry Orchard and all the streets he could think of, as many times as possible to divert him and make his account so real that even a dying man would see its truth – though hoping that by a miracle the talismanic words would save his life.

'It's on'y one you killed, sarge,' he whispered. 'Don't much matter.'

After dark Nevill dragged him a few feet at a time. 'Find somebody else,' Clifford said. 'I'm finished. I'll never be old.'

Nevill had to get someone back to safety. 'Don't talk so bleddy daft.'

He carried him a yard or two, thinking that as long as he hung on to him he need never consider the hangman again. He sweated grit and spat blood and pissed sulphur – as the saying went – and knew he was always close to conking out.

'Why are we in a tunnel, sergeant?' Clifford's eyes filled with soil and tears. 'Yer off yer sodding nut. Yer pulling your guts out for nowt.'

Occasional rifle shots sounded, but the machine guns and artillery had ceased. 'They'll hang me,' he said. 'Shut up.'

Clifford pulled both legs into his chest, choking on his blood. 'They'll shoot me, without me rifle. I don't like this tunnel, though. We went over the top, didn't we, not in a tunnel. Must a bin a mistake.'

He knelt close and saw his face in the light of a flare. 'Yes, we did go over the top, and you're wounded, you fool, so shut your mouth.' He whispered into his ear as he lay down beside him: 'A real Blighty one yer've got. You'll be out of it for *good* soon.'

English voices called low in the darkness, and stretcher-bearers found them. When they pulled at Nevill's arm to part him from Jack Clifford he screamed in agony.

The adjutant went through the rolls at Battalion Headquarters and said: 'Sergeant Nevill? Wasn't he the one we sent the signal for? Don't suppose he got it in time. All they wanted was for him to come back and explain why he had indented for too many ration replacements last week. We'd have put him down for a medal, bringing in a wounded man like that while he was wounded himself, if only the chap hadn't died.'

When Nevill was demobbed in the spring of 1919 he went back to Nottingham and found Amy. She had her own small house, and took him in as if he'd just come back from shooting rabbits in Robins Wood. Three months later she was pregnant again, and he was already at work on a mechanic's job that was to last thirty years. He looked after Amy and her first son, and then she had two by him, but he was never brave enough to tell her what he told Jack Clifford near Gommecourt. He was on the point of it often, but sensed that if he let it out they wouldn't stay together any more.

Those good souls who helped old Nevill from the table in The Radford Arms averred he was no more than a bag of skin and bone. He trembled as they sat him down, and the landlord nodded at one of his bar-keepers to bring a dash of whisky and water. It had already passed closing time, and two more men who were also good enough to order him something were forced to drink it themselves.

'Funny bloody story he was trying to spin us,' one of them said, 'about killing somebody in Robins Wood.'

'Couldn't make head nor tail of it. I've known him years, and he wouldn't hurt a fly. A bit senile, I suppose. Come on, get that turps down your throat, then we'll drive him back to his missis in Beaconsfield Terrace.'

Nevill thought he would have a word or two if ever he met Jack Clifford again about the secret he'd foisted on him but which nobody else had taken notice of when he let it out in the boozer. Not that he had much of a wait before discovering whether or not he'd see old Jack. Nobody was surprised when old Amy found him dead one morning, sitting fully dressed by the fireplace. Having heard about his dancing on the table in the pub, the neighbours had supposed – as they said at the funeral – that it couldn't be long after that.